C O N F I D E N C E

CONFIDENCE

STORIES

RUSSELL SMITH

A
JOHN METCALF
BOOK

BIBLIOASIS
WINDSOR, ONTARIO

Library and Archives Canada Cataloguing in Publication

Smith, Russell, 1963-, author
Confidence / Russell Smith.

Short stories.
Issued in print and electronic formats.
ISBN 978-1-77196-015-1 (pbk.). — ISBN 978-1-77196-016-8 (ebook)

I. Title.

PS8587.M58397C65   2015   C813'.54   C2014-907955-9
C2014-907956-7

Edited by John Metcalf
Cover and text design by Gordon Robertson
Cover photo: Shapes #1 (Self-Portrait, 2008 Series),
by Sandrine Carole Photographic Design
Copy-edited by Emily Donaldson

Biblioasis acknowledges the ongoing financial support of the Government of
Canada through the Canada Council for the Arts, Canadian Heritage, the Canada
Book Fund; and the Government of Ontario through the Ontario Arts Council.

PRINTED AND BOUND IN CANADA

RECYCLED
Paper made from
recycled material
FSC
www.fsc.org   FSC® C103567

For Hugo Smith

CONTENTS

CRAZY

H E DIDN'T CALL Emma's friend Claudia till he got to a bar and had something reddish and harsh in front of him. Actually he didn't call Claudia until the second reddish thing was in front of him; he drank the first one in three burns. His eyes were stinging from it when he called Claudia. And then when he spoke to her, calmly but with that tone of resignation or melancholy that he knew to sound brave, and gave her an update, the colours of the bar were quickly strong, the lights lush. He said, "No, she's still in hospital. They're keeping her overnight." He gulped again.

Booze smells of sugar, and this place smelled of sugar and flowers and hot rushes of coffee. It swirled. There were women behind the bar and around him, leaning and picking up glasses and telephones as if instructed to do so by a director with smutty intent; they were posing as women. Their shirts were riding up to show stripes of brown flesh, their skirts had slits or their jeans showed obvious subterranean ridges. They all had lives that involved dressing up and going to work and no mandatory and unpredictable hours in psychiatric wards.

"I just got out now," he said. "I've been there all day, more than all day, since about four in the morning." It was six-thirty in the evening now. "Yes, ambulance, police, the whole bit. In the bathroom, she was. No, she hadn't actually hurt herself, she was just, you know, threatening. For hours, yes."

There were screens, too, above the bar and behind him, showing films and loops carefully chosen for their incongruity—for it was that sort of bar, a curated bar, with clever names for cocktails—and those screens with their ancient cartoons or rotating polyhedra absorbed his vision even more than the stretching women did. It was a place of total distraction, the throbbing caricatural inverse of the waiting room in the ward. He could still feel the energy-saving fluorescent light on his skin like a scent. His eyes had been dulled by grey and now they were awake.

"No, Kee is with her, her friend Kee, from the support group. And she's calmer now, of course, the first thing they do is sedate them. But Kee has to go at seven, she has to work, so I'm going right back there now. I just have to eat something that isn't in a wrapper from a machine." He took another mouthful of burning syrup, wagged his head no to the waitress who had pointed at a menu. She smiled back at him and he noted that. He closed his eyes and saw the pile of wrappers on the side table in the ward waiting room: the mustardy sandwiches, the french fries. He had had coffee and Coke and Five Alive.

"Thank you, no," he said to Claudia, "we'll be fine. I'm guessing they'll let her out first thing in the morning and I'll bring her home. And she's usually okay then. I know you're working too. No, I'm fine." He tried to laugh. "I'm used to it. And her mom and her sister are coming now. Yes, now."

He listened to Claudia for a while telling him how good he was, and then he stopped listening because she was getting weepy and repetitively apologetic that she couldn't have been there but it was her work she couldn't do anything about, she was already on probation from missing too many hours with her fibromyalgia which was playing up again. He watched the screen that was now playing a science fiction movie he remembered from his childhood and it brought back being home from school sick and the smell of the basement rec room.

"I don't know what brought it on, honestly," he said, when she asked him a second time. "It's usually nothing. She gets these ideas. It's usually something she suspects I did, like I did something illicit. I don't know, like I've been taking drugs or having an affair with the girl at the corner store. No, not her specifically, I mean someone like her. Actually there is an obese Portuguese man who runs my corner store."

But Claudia was waiting for him to tell her exactly who had been suspected, so he said, "Oh, this time it was someone I work with. You don't know her. I have to have meetings with her sometimes, she called after supper one time, at the house, and that was it, from that moment, she was, you know. And everything I did from that moment—this was only about a week ago—every single thing was evidence, it was a secret conversation, and everything I said or did with my face was a hint, it was a clue."

He sighed because it was tiring to tell this and he had hoped not to have to go into such detail. He had gone into this detail several times with two doctors, or three, depending on how you counted the teams of people you waited for in a barred cage and then gave the same account to. Then you watched them leave and you were alone again for two or three hours with someone who was sobbing or sleeping or demanding to leave or trying to break the opaque glass of the observation room or trying to plan a holiday or wondering which of your friends might want to ask Katy or Claudia out or saying that she knew all along that you had not loved her. And you were then thinking about how better you could tell your story to the next team of apparently concerned young people who came in. (The teams of young people, he wanted to tell Claudia, were perfectly multi-racial and gender-balanced, as if selected for a commercial, which was probably not, if you thought about it, a statistical representation of the city's population but rather of the highly driven children-of-immigrants population, and all that was interesting but not, probably, to Claudia at this moment.)

"Anyway," he said, "then she gets, I guess, demanding. She gets to have something right away, like a kid, a child, with a toy, like a really young child. You know when they just have to have this one toy and they scream. So in this case it was, she wanted me to do something for her, something ridiculous, she wanted me to drive her somewhere, to see this woman's house, to see exactly where she lived, so that she could watch it, or whatever, I don't know exactly what she wanted to do, I kept asking her."

He looked at his watch; this was almost over, he would have to walk through the idyllic little park and across the intersection to the stern hospital. He had no time to tell this story, but once you started with the details it was hard to truncate.

"So I kept saying no, I'm not going to participate in something so crazy, and she wouldn't let it go. She was just sobbing a lot at first and threatening and saying all the dark things, you know, about using again or cutting, but I didn't take it seriously, and then the phone rang and I didn't answer it and of course it was an unknown number so that convinced her, for sure, that there was a secret and someone was calling for me, and then I walked out and I came back in and she was out on the balcony, and she was naked—no, nothing, completely—and she was starting to climb over and I had to wrestle with her, you know we're ten floors up, and, yeah. Yes, it was really. It was dangerous. Then I got her into bed and then I was calling the ambulance on the phone and then I came back in and I pulled back the sheet and she had a pair of little scissors, nail scissors, in there and she was, no, not cutting, just sort of scratching, but. You know. And then you know when you call an ambulance for that they have to send police too, so we had the whole thing, the whole scene, with all the neighbours out in the hallway and everything. And she was screaming, oh yeah."

He rubbed his face with his palm as if it would wipe away the rictus he knew was there. There was laughter around him.

"And then when we got there she tried to leave and the door was locked and that made her freak out even more, and then they had to restrain her to do toxicology, with the actual straps, the leather straps, like a movie about a loony bin, so that took about four, no six hours, all told, because there were different doctors, and waiting for the results. They made me wait outside for that, for the restraining, which is just as well, because I couldn't have watched. I have to go back now." He waved at the smiley waitress for his bill. "No, the blood work was clean. Nothing. But you know, after sedating her they just send her home, they don't set anything up. There's no follow-up. They say she has to just make an appointment to see her regular shrink, who is away on holiday, of course, and she won't go to see her anyway and I can't make her. Okay. I know. Thanks. Yes, call tomorrow."

Claudia had to go suddenly. Perhaps she was exhausted by the story.

He made two more calls: to Philip at the trust he worked for about why he hadn't written the minutes from the donors' committee meeting or priced the marquee or the caterer for the Red Ball as he had been supposed to do by the end of the day. He knew he was leaving this message at the exact moment Philip would have turned off his phone for his run.

Then he called the roofer and left another message saying that the sliding door was still leaking and there was a pool starting inside the bathroom window too. He reminded the roofer, who also did not answer his phone, that the roofer had promised he would be there that day and the day before and he reminded the roofer that the condo corporation's lawsuit against the developer was coming to the negotiation phase and that the insurance company had already said they would cover it so this was a no brainer job.

He did not then call the condo association lawyer for an update.

When he put his phone in his pocket he never wanted to hear or touch a telephone again in his life.

It was spring in the little park, cold and bright green, with the smell of weed from the teenagers on the monkey bars that rendered him yearning and a little weepy again.

He went through the emergency entrance and nodded at the guard who recognized him and buzzed him through. Then he stood at the armoured door of the psych ward and looked in at the waiting room, which had by then been cleared of his fast food wrappers. The waiting room had two new inhabitants, a black lady and her mad daughter who was large, maybe six feet tall, with hair she had obviously cropped herself, and men's clothes. The daughter was standing in the middle of the room and talking to someone invisible. Her mother was sitting still and looking at the floor with practiced patience. She had a handbag on her lap, and a hat with a brim.

He had to buzz a couple of times before anyone came out. The young people in their green scrubs moved very slowly on this ward, as if reluctant to help anyone, he didn't know why. They were all cold and suspicious and asked you everything three times to see if you were lying.

They took him to the little room where she was. It was a cubicle with a sliding glass door you could close which had no curtain. There was no window.

She was sleeping on her side. Her thick hair. The room smelled sweaty. They had not given her a gown or any change of clothes. The soles of her feet, pushed out from under the synthetic blanket, were dirty.

A fat woman who was not wearing hospital clothes came in. They all had dangling i.d. cards at their waists but how could you read them? How could you know if anyone was a doctor or a janitor? She shook Emma's shoulder and told her briskly her husband was here.

Emma turned and blinked at him and slowly sat up. She looked around with something like curiosity. She did not seem alarmed. "Are we going?"

"No, sweetie, they're going to keep you a little longer. You're going to sleep here."

"I'm not sleeping here any more," she said without energy.

He did not reply to this and she didn't push it. They had been on this subject all day.

"Would you like something to eat?" said the fat lady.

Emma nodded. The lady padded out.

Emma didn't look at him. She pushed her hair behind her ears and looked at her nails. She was wearing a tight little tank top thing with spaghetti straps and no bra and of course she looked sexy, how could she not, how could she not know. This was part of it, for sure, this flaunting of her breasts and little body. For a second he hated her for it.

He said, "It's good that you're hungry. A good sign. It's good to eat."

She was silent for a while. He waited.

She said, "I'm sorry."

He nodded.

She said, "I'm so, so sorry. I'm really sorry. I mean it. I am."

She said this for a while and then said she knew how she had ruined his whole day and his whole week and she didn't know how he would ever forgive her. And that she would make it up to him, and that she knew now that none of those things was so important, those things that had stressed her out, and it didn't matter if anything was true or not true, what was important was that she had him and he was so nice and he always took care of her and she was really, truly sorry, and she really felt a lot better and thought she could go home now.

He scraped his chair closer and took her hand while she said this, and then he stroked her forearm. "We'll see what they say," he said.

She said, "How's your friend Erik?"

"Erik? I'm not sure. I haven't—why?"

"I'm wondering if he would be interested in Claudia. She's kind of artistic, like him."

CONFIDENCE

Then her mother and her sister were there, standing in the doorway, in their raincoats, and they went first to him and embraced him and then sat beside her on the bed and in his chair and stroked her hands and asked her if she was feeling better and if they had given her anything to eat.

Her mother then couldn't resist asking her what had so upset her in the first place and he said, quietly, "I don't know if we want to talk about that right now."

"I always say the wrong thing," her mother said.

"We don't need to fight right now," said her sister.

"Did you bring my iPod?" said Emma.

"It wasn't on the table," said her sister. "It wasn't anywhere."

"It was right sitting there on the little hall table just inside the front door. You couldn't miss it."

"Well I looked there and it wasn't there."

"You're going to need to sleep anyway," said her mother.

"It was just one small thing. The only thing I asked you to bring," said Emma.

"You should go home," her sister said to him. "You need a rest. Go home and sleep."

He looked at Emma. "You'll be okay if I go sleep? With these guys here?"

"Of course." Emma reached her arms out to him and closed her eyes. He leaned down and embraced her. Her smell of slept-in sheets.

The fat woman arrived with a tray with a sandwich of white bread and a sealed cup of juice and a styrofoam bowl of soup. There was a banana and a rice pudding. It was so forlorn it almost made him cry again.

Emma looked at it without response, but she reached for the sandwich.

"Okay," he said. "I'm going to go."

"You are the best," she said. "You are so good. I love you."

Her mother and sister both stood and embraced him at the door. They both whispered thanks in his ear and they both said they were sorry, as if it were their fault, but more likely because neither of them could have come earlier.

"You are a rock," said her mother to him. "A rock."

"I don't know why everyone's so upset," said Emma. "I'm fine. I should just go now and then everyone could go too."

No one responded to this.

In the corridor he asked the fat woman, "So how long are you going to keep her?"

"Oh that's not up to me. That will be up to the doctor."

"I thought you were a doctor."

"No dear."

"So what does the doctor think?'

"We're waiting for the doctor now. He hasn't seen her yet."

"We've been here about twelve hours. She's been interviewed by so many people I can't . . . So which doctor are we waiting for now?"

"The supervising doctor. He still has to see her."

"Okay. So when might that be?"

She shook her head. "Any time. We really don't know. We're all waiting for him now."

"So you mean it could be like all night?"

"Could be. Probably not. He'll be here."

He left her with his phone number and then he was out on the dark street. The cold was enlivening.

He walked straight back to the same bar and ordered a beer. He tried to look at the menu. The smiley bartender came over and spread her hands along the bar. "You're back," she said as if pleased by this charming and unlikely occurrence.

"I am back." And he smiled back with the filling sense that there were some relationships with women you could have that were friendly and civilized and mutually beneficial, that you could in fact talk to them and express views and hear responses just as you could with anyone and this was more normal than not normal and in fact an activity that was going on all around him. He wondered what the key to this was, besides perhaps never sleeping with them. He wondered if the key was perhaps maintaining the fiction, in your relationships with them, that there were no other women in your acquaintance, that you did not have to work with women, did not know any, were not even aware that women existed in the universe. He wondered how long it would take him, what simple thing he would have to say, to make this friendly bartender announce that he obviously hated her and that she was going to New Zealand to work on an organic farm with people who had ideals. He could probably get it to happen within half an hour if all he did was express an opinion about something.

He said, "I'm back. I would like to eat something. I can't read this menu. Feed me something."

She stared at him for a second, then said, "All right. You trust me?"

"I more than trust you. I am excited by the idea of you feeding me."

She slid down the bar and tapped things onto her screen. She said to him, "You're getting some pulled pork sliders and an avocado quinoa salad."

"Delicious. You have seen right into my soul."

"Are you okay for drinks?'

"This one seems to be defective."

"Defective?"

"It is flawed by insufficiency. I would like a replacement."

She brought him another pint. It was dark, meaty-looking. He drank it with energy. Before she turned away he said, "I would like to see into your soul now too."

"Yup," she said, quite quickly, "so do a lot of gentlemen at this bar."

"Oh." He was scalded by this. He tried to keep his smile, which now felt stiff. "Not gentlemen quite like me, though, surely."

"Gentlemen quite like you, yes."

He looked at his beer and let her walk away. Now he didn't want his pulled pork and pretentious salad. He never would have ordered a salad made of grains anyway.

He waited a minute more and then, when she had turned to someone else, put two bills down on the counter. He took a last look at her tight jeans and the bare waist and the furrows of her bra strap, and he left.

He walked for quite a few blocks, not towards home. He knew where he was going: it was a place up a flight of dark stairs on a street of dollar stores and Ethiopian grocers. His heart raced as he approached the doorway, and he even stopped for a moment and tried to get himself to go home. But he kept walking, glanced around quickly before pushing open the door marked only with a number, and plodded up the stairs.

At the top was a closed door and a bell. You had to push it and wait there, breathing hard, for someone to come and look at you through the peephole and open the door.

The door opened and it was a chubby Russian. She had her clunky heels on and her little sparkly dress with a zipper up the front. She said "Yes can I help you?" as they have to do and he mumbled that he had been there before and knew Jessamyn. She took him through to a room with a sofa and a TV screen. She asked him how long he wanted to stay and he gave her two more bills for a half hour. He sat on the sofa. She brought in another girl and the two of them stood in front of him.

This was the awkward part, one he had never liked. The Russian was blonde and caramelly, with large breasts pumped up under her chin. The other was pale, black-haired, also puffy, with high black boots and a black dress. He could see lace stocking tops under the dress.

"Are you interested in blue room or red room?" said the Russian. "I am blue room, which has soft bed, like spa, and relax, and Samara is red room, which has more specialize, if you like more special, with chair and table."

He looked at the one called Samara, saw her leather wristband with its big chrome buckle, the hint of confinement, and this decided him. He nodded at her. The other lady smiled and darted away. "This way," said Samara, very softly, as if unenthusiastic, which was, he supposed, not surprising.

She took him to a little room with a shower and a futon on the floor and low lamps with red shades. There was a leather-covered bench and a closed wardrobe. It smelled very sweet, like raspberry soap. Samara said she would be right back if he would like to have a shower.

Taking off your clothes in these rooms was like a medical procedure: there was the same lack of space, the same hurry, and the same sense that one's clothes were ugly when piled up on a chair, that they looked dirty and should be hidden somehow. The water in the shower was not quite hot.

He lay on the bed with a towel over his crotch as you would wait for an X-ray. He had spent a lot of the day waiting.

She knocked and opened the door, just as a doctor would. She said, "How are you doing this evening?"

She sat on the edge of the bed and stroked his thigh. "What can I do for you this evening? How about a relaxing massage?"

He considered this. A part of him actually wanted a massage.

"Really," he said, "I'm looking for you to just . . . take care of me. Tell me what you want me to do."

"You want me," she said very softly, "to take control?"

Her fingers were playing higher on his thigh. He could smell body lotion and the memory of a cigarette, which was not an unarousing combination.

"Yes."

"Are you looking for like a special service?"

"I guess so, yes."

"You want me to treat you a little rough?"

He said "Yes" and he began to sweat.

"You want me to treat you like a bad boy?"

He exhaled, not liking this language.

"Is there any particular equipment that interests you?"

There was a squeaking sound, some hissing. His phone, trying to play a tune.

He said "I have to get that," and he sat up and then stood up and searched his pants for it. He felt aware of her looking at him as he bent over, his thin legs and his balls dangling.

"Hello?"

"Hi."

"Emma? Emma. What's up?"

"Well, they're letting me go."

He turned to make apologetic gestures at Samara. She shrugged and looked at the floor.

He said, "Letting you go? Letting you go? Why?"

"What do you mean why? Because I'm fine is why."

"Did the doctor come to see you?"

"He just said I was fine and I could go. Not that I could go, actually, that I had to go, because they have no space for me and this is an acute ward and not a long-term facility and blah blah."

"Jesus."

"What's wrong? What are you doing?"

"Nothing, I'm—" He put his hand over the mouthpiece and shook his head at Samara. He put one finger in the air. She nodded and left the room, closing the door with a click.

"Where are you?" said Emma.

"I'm just walking. I walked for miles." He was shaking his pants out, sticking one leg in, wriggling. "Where's your mom and Liz?"

"Well I sent them home. There was no reason for them to be here."

"Okay. Okay. So I'll have to get home. To get the car. I'll come and get you. So just relax. I'll be right there." He had his shirt over one arm. "Okay? Will they let you wait there?"

"Yes."

"I'm coming."

"You are so sweet. I'm sorry."

When he was dressed he opened the door and listened in the dim corridor. He heard a radio or a TV. Samara came out of another door.

"I'm very sorry," he said. "I have to go." He stepped back into the room and took out his wallet. He gave her three twenties and apologized again and she seemed happy with that.

When he got her home she turned on the TV and sat as if nothing had happened. She had been talkative in the car, wanting to know how his friends Colm and Raj were, if they had girlfriends yet, and if either of them would consider dating Katy, who had been calling her and who was really very smart despite her obvious craziness.

There was no message on the phone from the roofer, or from the condo association lawyer, but there was one from Philip his boss saying that if there was anything he needed to be told about he was always willing to lend an ear.

He called her mom and told her she was home and her mom said she was so relieved and happy for him that she was okay and so grateful that she had someone like him, someone so solid and patient and dependable. She told him again he was a rock.

He went into the room where she was watching TV and the TV was off and she was folded up on the sofa and sobbing.

He sat next to her, stroked her shoulder.

Then he got up and went into the bathroom and locked the door. From under the sink he took a box of tissues and pulled the tissues out. From under the tissues he extracted a plastic bottle, and from the bottle he took two white pills. He put the pills on the sink counter and used the heel of the bottle to crush them

to powder. He took the cardboard from a packet of pink dispos-
able razors and used it to corral the powder into ridges. Then he
rolled the cardboard into a tube and snorted both lines. There was
a stinging and then a dizziness.

He wiped up the counter and tore the cardboard into smaller
strips and threw it away. he put the bottle back into the tissue box,
noting that there were only seven pills remaining and that he
would have to make an arrangement to meet Danny or someone
like him this weekend. This made him so anxious he almost pulled
the bottle out again. Danny had been in and out of town and was
not always available, and he would have to make risky phone calls
to find another guy like Danny and then, who knows, with the cur-
rent supply situation, how much people were charging or whether
they were trying to sell you the new substitute appropriately called
Neo like some kind of satire. If he had to start paying a hundred
bucks a pill he would not be able to continue, and all the solutions
to this were unthinkable.

He went back to where she was and sat and waited for the nausea to pass and the calm to reach him.

She put her head on his shoulder. "I'm so sorry," she wept, "this
shouldn't happen to you. You're so good. You're so perfect. You
don't deserve it."

He just patted her. "Everything's okay now. You're home. You
have to stop worrying so much about everything." His arms were
heavy and he yawned. He felt the cold spreading through him
now. Soon she would be asleep and then so would he.

She was crying so hard now she was almost shrieking. "I don't
know. I don't even know what I would do. Without you. You're so
good to me. What would I do? What would I do?"

He looked at the window that had no blind or covering on it,
so that all you could see in it was your own room, your red lamp,
the blue TV. There was a railing running the length of it outside,
a bar, to prevent any of the windows from opening. The place was
perfectly sealed off. There would be no going outside again now.

RESEARCH

S HE READ, "And thought about things. Sometimes he thought sadly to himself, Why? and sometimes he thought, Wherefore? and sometimes he thought, Inasmuch as which?"

He smiled at this, lying there in the darkness, mostly because of her accent, which was American and all wrong. It was like hearing it through some kind of distortion filter, or FX box. He could smell the smoke in her hair. He breathed it in.

"And sometimes he didn't quite know what he was thinking about. So when Winnie-the-Pooh came stumping along, Eeyore was." She read slowly, sometimes tripping and starting again.

He had his eyes closed and his hand on her back, which was bare. He was trying to feel the tattoos under his hand. She was reading by one candle and by the streetlamp glow that came in from between the battered slats of the blind and made her body a pale glow, a white smudge. You could just make out the black stripes like wings on her back. But he was trying to feel them with his fingertips. He didn't want any light to disturb the room, which was very still.

She read very softly. "Not very how he said. I don't seem to have felt at all how for a long time. Dear dear said Pooh."

Her accent was from southern Florida, a place he pictured as parking lots and air-conditioned diners. He kept his eyes closed.

He was hoping he wouldn't cry. It would be embarrassing. His foot was twitching a little but his body was still. It was a mixed up feeling, what he felt: this miraculous calm, to be with her here and having her soothe him like this, the sick joy of being cradled, the sickness he felt at realizing the pleasure he was seeking was his own childhood. He could not stop smiling, though. And he would probably cry, at some point.

He knew the patterns on her back were thick and sharp-edged, either wings or blades. His fingertips slid up and down the dunes of her ribs. The sweat on them had cooled. Her voice was breathy in his ear.

"Let's have a look, said Eeyore, and he turned slowly round to the place where his tail had been a little while ago." She giggled a little.

He slid his face along the pillow and kissed her shoulder. There was a black star on it. He kissed the dark star.

She reached for the bottle on the floor and gulped some water. Then she put her palm to his forehead. Her palm was hot. She said to his forehead, "Are you asleep?"

He said to her neck, "It will be light out any second."

"Don't think about it."

"That was lovely."

She closed the book gently. "I've started saying that now. Lovely. Everything is lovely."

"You don't like it?"

"It's ridiculous. Lovely. I should wear a straw hat and flowers to say that."

He ran his hand along her thigh. "I think it's a lovely word."

She kissed him.

He said, "I want it to be dark for a while longer. I'd rather fall asleep in the dark."

"It's still dark."

"I don't want to see the light yet."

She said, "Are you sleepy?"

"Nnnn. Not really."

Their faces were very close and they were speaking in murmurs just above a whisper. Her eyes were blazing black. She said, barely moving her lips, "Me neither."

He put his fingertips to her throat, felt the pulse.

He said, "I'm still twitchy."

"Did you sleep at all, just now?"

"A little, I guess. It's that sleep and not asleep thing. It's a kind of halfway."

"I know."

There was a slightly different texture to the darkness now in the corners of the room; it was thinning, slipping away like sleep when you wake. He looked at the blind and wondered if he could fix the slats so that no dawn could get in at all. "Do you want to get up?"

"No."

He said, "At least I've stopped grinding."

"Me no."

"Really?"

"I probably will all day and next day. It always happens."

"That sucks."

He dropped his hands from her neck and they fell away from each other, onto their backs. Their hands were still touching. The candle flickered on the ceiling. The room was definitely paler, a greyer light. It was beginning to end. He said, "This is silly, how mushy I feel."

"I feel it too."

"It's just chemicals," he said.

"No, it's not." She rolled towards him and they kissed again, their lips cool and dry now. He couldn't stop touching her, just letting his fingers brush her little breasts, the edge of her ears. This was how they were going to talk from now on, he imagined, kissing every three words. It would be tiring, but he couldn't stop.

He said, "So are you really okay now?"

"I told you. I'm fine. I was fine right away. I just . . . it was too hot and I couldn't breathe. It was only for a second."

"I was so scared. When I saw you go down on the sidewalk. It was like a, like a tower collapsing."

She said, "I'm really, really sorry."

"Stop saying that. It's fine. I've said this how many times now."

"I worry that you think I did it deliberately, that I was just playing a game to get you out of there, and . . ."

"Of course not. Stop this. I didn't think that for a second. I'm just happy you're okay. I saw you come out of the bathroom and you were white, white. I knew something was wrong. So I followed you out onto the sidewalk and when I saw you go down, my heart, my belly just went cold, I thought, oh fuck, this could be really bad. I saw the paramedic coming over."

She said, "What were they doing there anyway?"

"They just wait outside these things. The promoters have to have them on hand. It's a by-law. It's in case what happened happens. They're there exactly for girls like you."

"For girls who didn't eat enough. I'm sorry."

"Next time I'll watch you eat before you go."

She said, "I'm sorry. You spent so much money on everything."

"Shut up. I was so scared when I saw you go down. You just went down on one knee and you sort of keeled over and coiled up. It was very graceful. I was glad you didn't hit your head."

"I don't remember anything. I don't even remember coming out of the bathroom."

They had already been through this, but he knew that they would have to go on telling the story a few times. They had to go over it carefully. It had been scary. And now it was over. He said, "You came and got me and you were white and stumbling and I followed you. And then you came to right away and the paramedic was there and he was being kind of aggressive, and he said he couldn't let you back in until he examined you, and I knew we weren't going back in right then. I had all these pictures of me explaining to your parents why you were in the hospital, and then to the cops, and then to the papers . . ."

"I remember sitting on the sidewalk and drinking water. And then I was fine."

"It wasn't your fault. It was awful in there. And there was a weird energy."

"There was an aggression. It's true. It was weird. Girls were being super weird in the bathroom."

"Really?"

"They were pounding on the door of the stall when I was just hanging on in there, I thought I would puke, and they were banging and yelling."

"I saw that one girl push you when you came out. Who the hell were those people?"

"They were all dressed funny. It was some promotion."

He closed his eyes so as to not see the gathering light. It was definitely grey in the room now. He said, "It was beer, I think. Or some kind of cooler. They had bright green shorts and tank tops.

She said, "The tank tops were white."

"Their skin was all dark and orange. And the boys with them, the boys were like club boys from Richmond Street, they were huge and had big shirts and gold chains. I don't know what the fuck they were doing in there."

She said, "It was like some massive don't."

He laughed. "There were some really bad don'ts in there. Did you see the little guy with a straw hat? A little straw hat, a boater, like an impressionist painting."

"I saw him. That was a girl."

"I know. That's what I was going to tell you."

She placed a hand flat on the bottom of his belly, her fingers on the crease of his thigh. He tensed his stomach. She played with his curls and he pushed against her. She said, "That kind of makes it a do."

"I know. It's totally different. It's hard to tell. There's such a fine line."

"The caption would read, 'You know how sometimes you see a little guy all brazen with a cool hat like this in the wrong place and you say good for you? And then you realize it's a chunky chick and you think, oh, that's totally different, but you don't know if it's good or bad?'"

He rolled over and buried his face in her hair. The room was not dark any more. The blind glowed.

He said, "It's too bad we had already dropped the pills. We could have slept."

"It was fun in the park, though, no?"

"It was. It was super fun. It was lovely. I liked just walking with you on the grass. All those kids hiding in the bushes, kissing."

"The swings were fun."

"And the light was so weird. That fluorescent light that made the leaves so green and unnatural. It was like a magic park. It felt secret. I guess we were high."

She said, "That was a good thing to do."

"Yes."

"What are we going to do today?"

He rolled onto his back. "You want to spend the day with me?"

"Yes."

"Okay."

She said, "Are you sick of me?"

And this gave him a paroxysm of the physical tension that was like a pain in him, a rush of blood to the groin and an ache in the prostate. He couldn't not grab her; it was like glue, he wanted to stick to her, be in her, to be her. He was stiff and pushing against her.

She pushed against him too. They kissed but their mouths were dry. So it faded. It had been coming and going like this.

He said, "We have to go somewhere quiet and calm, like nature."

"Nature?"

And then they laughed at the idea of nature, of finding nature there. He thought of Southern Florida. He imagined her when she lived there, walking on barbed wire to get to school, hitchhiking in trucks, being pulled on a skateboard by sportscars: her life had been a movie. He had not been there; he could not imagine it.

He said, "I know. It will have to be a park or something. Or we could leave the city."

"Like where?"

"We could go to, I don't know, a place with a lake, or a beach or something."

"They're all far. You mean rent a car?"

"What time do you have to be home."

She hesitated a moment before saying, "Around six."

He too was silent for a moment before saying, "Okay, that's plenty of time. We could go."

"Where?"

"I don't know. I don't know nature."

"Maybe it's too far."

He said, "High Park?"

"Sure."

"It's a holiday today. It will be full of families."

"It's a holiday?"

"Yes."

"Oh."

"What about the lake? Just walk along the lake."

"Okay."

She grabbed his hand and their noses touched. And then they were just staring into each other's eyes in the stuffy dawn light of the room, like some kind of movie, and they both knew it was silly and a cliché, but because of the drugs—and they knew this, they knew it was because of the drugs—it wasn't silly. He also knew that it was different because of the drugs, because something had happened; it meant something now. He wondered if she knew this too.

She said, in a very small voice, "We're going to do this?"

"We're going to. We're going to walk along the lake together."

Her eyes were shiny. She turned away and rubbed her face.

He said, very quietly, almost in a whisper, "We're in trouble now, you know."

"What?"

"You heard me."

She was leaning over the edge of the bed. She found a tissue and blew her nose. She said, "You say I'm in trouble?"

"No. We're in trouble."

"I thought that's what you said. What do you mean?"

"I mean. This is bonding. This isn't just a fling any more."

She lay very still. Then she picked up the Winnie-the-Pooh and started turning the pages. He knew she wasn't reading it.

She said, "What's the holiday?"

"It's Canada Day. I think."

"What's that?"

"It's a holiday. I don't know."

"I hate holidays. Everything's closed."

He said, "I know. It's weird. You go out and you're walking along and you realize something is weird. And then you figure out it's a holiday and everyone knew about it and how did they know about it? Do they announce it in the paper or something?"

"It's in calendars."

"Who reads calendars?"

"They have jobs."

"Oh," he said. "Jobs. Right."

She put the book away and lay her head on his chest. And for some reason in the light they felt they could sleep again and they drifted off, probably only for a few minutes. He had a brief dream about his former high school: the images were transparent, as if bleached, lit from behind. He woke; it was the daylight coming in.

They woke together and fell apart. It was getting hot in the room. There was a bird outside. He pushed the covers off her.

Her body was long and white. The black rivers on her back didn't extend to her front. There was only the winged thing in the centre of her chest (which she said she hated now and which she wanted to get rid of, but which he thought was thrilling and beautiful), and the ring of flames or leaves around her ankle. The tattoos were exactly the same black as her pubic hair. Her hipbones jutted like tent poles. He put a hand on one, felt its edge. He said, "You have to eat more."

She put a pillow over her head.

He closed his eyes and felt sleep drifting near and far again. When he opened his eyes he didn't know if he had been asleep, or how long they had been lying this way. He said, "Are you hungry yet?"

"No."

"We should try to eat something."

"Why?"

"Or have juice, anyway. Juice is good."

"Okay."

"Let's get up and have juice."

"No. Not yet." She grabbed him and held on, her head on his chest.

He played with the black hair snaking over his skin. He said, "We have to get up at some point. It's starting to get hot."

"Okay."

She kicked the sheet off her ankles and stood, long and wavy, then tottered for a second, as if dizzy. She held on to the dresser. He watched her, ready to get up. Then she straightened and glided soundlessly out the door, down the corridor.

He listened to the silver sound of her peeing and he loved even that. He loved that she was peeing in his toilet; he felt proud about it. He loved even more the fact that she had walked naked down the corridor; he had hoped for a second that his roommate would see her, how tall she was, and the tattoos cut out of her whiteness, but his roommate wasn't home, of course; he and Nula weren't back from the show yet, or perhaps they were at Nula's, or perhaps they had overheated and died in the crush. Perhaps they were dead.

He rose to his knees and parted the tattered venetian blind to look out the window: the fire escape, the alley, the bottles on the deck, the ashtray. They must have sat out there for an hour after they got back from the park. It looked like a different place entirely.

The sun was still buttery, but there was haze over the rooftops. He felt dry just looking at the light.

She was back in the room. She folded herself into the bed. They rolled and gripped each other, didn't move. Their hearts were still beating a little too fast.

They got up. They got dressed. They drank some juice but they couldn't eat either of the muffins that were in a cardboard box with a plastic top in the fridge.

They rode their bikes down to the lake.

They walked along the lake, sweating. The sky was yellow-grey, the air was steam. They were jostled by fat cyclists and rollerbladers in pads and helmets. She was wearing his T-shirt. Her feet were blistered from the stupid shoes she thought would be fun for dancing, blunt platform boots that went right up her calf, wrapped her in straps.

They wanted to hold hands but even their hands were too hot. They sat under a tree and drank water.

She said, "Maybe we're ready to sleep again."

"Yeah. Let's go home."

"I can't face the thought of cycling back."

"I know," he said, "Maybe we could leave our bikes here and take a cab."

"No."

They watched a couple lumber past, a man and a woman in tight cycling shorts. They both had fat white legs and little white socks, and wore sweatshirts that said things. One of the sweat-shirts had a wolf's face screened on it.

"Lots of don'ts," he murmured.

"Like can you even tell how old those people are? Are they twenty-five or forty-five? I have no idea."

"It's cool when you see old people together though."

"Not them though." There was a skinny guy in white pants. He was with a small Asian woman. He had his shirt open to show white chest hair. He wore white shoes made of woven leather. He was taking her picture in the grass.

"He got her mail-order. That's like a serious don't."

"There's a do." A roller-girl in small red shorts with a blue stripe up the side and a spandex crop-top. Her hair was in a long braid. She was moving fast.

"She's hot."

She said, "I always want to see what kind of guy they're with."

A big tanned guy with a shaved head came fast behind. "Okay," he said. "You like that?"

"Sure," she said. "For one night. But not really. He shaves his chest. I hate that."

"He must be gay."

"Gay might be a do, though."

"Gay might make him a do. Indeed."

"I'd prefer that to the long shorts guys called Dave and Todd and Mike."

"Hey Dave," he said, "We got tickets to the Red Hot Chili Pep-pers. Awesome. Outstanding. Hey Mike. Get you a frosty?"

"You're too good at that. Oh look."

A family of people who were definitely foreign, probably East-ern European, ushered children along the path. The older women had tight hairdos and smoked as they walked. One of them had stretchy pants that displayed the underwear cutting into her flesh. You could see the flowers on the underwear through the pants.

She said, "Wow."

He could say nothing else to this.

The youngest woman, who was pushing a pram, was tall and thin and had a pretty summer dress but wore knee-high flesh coloured stockings and plastic sandals.

"Wow," he said. "How can she ruin that dress with those stockings? That's so odd."

"Maybe it's cool. Like she doesn't care. I bet she doesn't shave her armpits."

"Oh," he said, "yeah, that is sexy. Smoky, sweaty Czechs with hairy armpits. That is kind of sexy."

Then they were sick and quiet. His mouth felt like sand.

She said, "Are you going to work today?"

He put his head on his knees. "No. No. I couldn't read. I don't even know if the library's open."

"What chapter are you working on?"

"Oh Christ. Is there any more water?"

She gave him the bottle and he finished it.

He said, " Something about mediation. It's about McLuhan, really, and Benjamin. I'm talking about early photography. But I'm not. I've been stuck on this chapter for months. Okay, that's really enough of that. I'm exhausted."

She said, "You want to watch *Until the End of the World* tonight?

"I thought you'd already seen it."

"I can watch it a million times. I want you to see it."

He was silent a long time. Then he said, "What time is Bob coming back?"

She sighed. "Some time today. It doesn't matter."

"I thought you said six."

"I have to go home for a bit. But I could come over later. I want to see this with you."

"Who's managing tonight?"

"Jerry. I don't know. Not me."

"When do you work next?"

"Tomorrow. Evening. I have nothing to do."

"But he'll be home tonight."

She shrugged. She put her head on her knees.

He said, "Don't you have to rejoin your real life at a certain point?"

She did not move, did not twitch. But after a time there were tears brimming in her eyes and falling out. Then she put her face in her hands.

"So," he said. "I said the wrong thing."

She got up. She walked briskly away.

He caught up with her at a railing on the lake. The water was flat and turgid. You could smell sewage. There were ducks just beneath them, swimming in floating oil. They were pecking at the cartons of food that had become stuck along the dock. One had a cigarette stuck in its feathers.

He said, "I'm sorry."

She said, "This water is just sludge. I can't believe they're swimming in it."

"Don't look down. Look out at the island."

She said, "Why did you have to say that?"

He said, "I don't know. To be mean, I guess."

"Why?"

"Because I got mad for a second. That we were pretending."

She let out a long shaky breath. "Okay."

"Sorry."

She said, "If you don't want to do this, if you can't handle it, we can stop. I've always said this. I've always said it would be difficult."

"I know. I can do this. I said I could do it."

She said, "What the hell are we going to do?" Her voice was wavering again.

He said, very low and calmly, "We're just going to wait until you've saved enough to move out."

"That's not till September."

"I can wait. It will be shitty until then."

She turned and kissed him quickly, then took his hand, and they walked towards their bikes.

They passed a guy wearing a shiny track suit that hung loosely on him; it looked like silk. He was Turkish or something. He looked like a sultan in a harem, except that his silks had meaningless words written on them, words in no language. Perhaps they were the name of a soccer team, or perhaps the name of the company that had made the clothes.

They both said "Do" at the same time.

He said, "Do you ever think about yours?"

"About my what?"

"About your thesis."

She shook her head. "I think that's. I'm not going to think about it any more."

She had studied pharmacology. That's why she had ended up in this city. But they had met at the Hound Bar, which Bob owned.

He thought of Bob, his moustache, his long hair, how on earth she had ever ended up with him. She had never explained. And what she was doing in that shitty restaurant. It was such a waste of her.

He decided he had to try to go to the library that afternoon, if only to sit in the coolness for a while, to tell himself he was there.

And back at his house, after the tears and the kisses and the promises, she rode off on her bicycle, in her big dancing boots, and he was relieved to be alone. He sat for a while and thought about watching a movie, but he was too hot, so he packed—trying to do it fast, without thinking, trying not to think about how little was left in the afternoon and how sleepy he would soon be—his laptop and some paper and his own copies of McLuhan and Benjamin, which he had not actually looked at for some weeks, and he got on his bike and rode in the haze to the library.

On Harbord Street he saw a middle aged guy with grey hair who was probably some computer game developer or TV guy, and this guy was wearing huge skater shorts that went down to his calf and exposed his birdy little ankles. He laughed, it was such a fantastic don't—this guy's name was probably Morton Feinbaum and he stayed home every night and watched American Idol and took notes on it with a dry seriousness and drove an Audi to his loft-like office every day—because he imagined telling all this to her, but then he was relieved that she wasn't there to see it and to hear him, because it had become kind of an addiction, this game, and it was all he thought about, and he had to think about something else. He couldn't stop it though: all he saw were don'ts. There was a girl in a kind of Laura Ashley sack dress, carrying books to the library. There was nothing but don'ts around him.

He found a post for his bike and had to take off his heavy knapsack to get his lock out. His T-shirt was already soaked. His knapsack was heavy because of the books he carried around, had been carrying around for several months now, like talismans, without reading them (although he had read them before, some passages several times, and already written essays about them). He felt sick lifting the bag off the ground and walking towards the library. He wondered if he would ever be rid of it. For a second he thought that the only thing worth doing with the books was to read them aloud to her, as she had read him Winnie-the-Pooh; they were a kind of prayer.

The library was silent and massive. It was mostly concrete; there was little glass in it. It looked like a fortress. It was never clear where the entrances were on the best of days, but on this one the basement door he normally used, under a staircase, was locked. There was no one on the grass pathways, no one on the streets. The heat of the day flattened the landscape, made the distance around to the far side of the building seem enormous, like walking in a desert. He had the illusion of walking on a treadmill without gaining ground.

He couldn't tell if the library was closed or open, so he wandered around its walls, trying doors, looking for a way in. When he realized he was too dazed to do so was when he knew, finally, that he was fooling himself, that he was never actually going to go in there again. He would move those books, though, from apartment to apartment, for the rest of his life.

FUN GIRLS

KATRINA lifted her leg, long as a hockey stick, flashing a sliver of gusset, and stuck it out the cab window. She did this to show the passing street her Italian boots, which had not attracted sufficient attention from Leona and Jennifer. "Do you like them? Milan. Aren't they lovely?"

"Do you think Timmy will be home?" said Jennifer, in the front.

"Who has a phone?" said Leona.

"I think they're beautiful," said Lionel. He sat between Katrina and Leona. He had his hand on the back of Katrina's neck, under her hair. Leona had one of her legs hooked over his, and was kissing him occasionally on the cheek, in a silly and sisterly way. He knew it didn't mean anything.

Jennifer, in the front, said, "No more kissing Lionel before I can have a chance too."

"Where are we going, love?" said Leona.

"I just love them," said Katrina, wiggling her ankle in the open window. "They're so soft."

"There were a lot of beautiful boots at that party," said Lionel. "You all have great boots."

"He is a good kisser," said Katrina.

"He's a *great* kisser," said Jennifer.

"I haven't had a real chance yet," said Leona.

"Not somewhere too fabulous," said Jennifer. "No fucking ghastly models. I haven't felt suicidal all day, not once."

"But sweetie, not somewhere too democratic, either, no beer bars or country music, all right? We have to compromise."

"Aren't you just dying for those fried crab ball things?" said Katrina. "Where were they?"

"Oh! At Sweet! I want those. I want to eat them. I want to eat them all up."

"So fabulous," said Jennifer. "Do you mind if I smoke? I know we're being terribly loud."

The driver smiled and shook his head uninterpretably, as if it would make any difference anyway, as Jennifer was already rolling down her window.

"What are you afraid of, sweetie? I don't know what she has against nice places. It's a phobia. It's a fabuphobia."

"I have no money," said Leona into Lionel's ear.

"That's what I have," said Jennifer, blowing out a stream of smoke. "Fabuphobia, that's exactly what I have."

"Is Sweet fabulous?" said Lionel.

"And I want the *gado-gado*, and fried wontons."

"So it's back three blocks," said Leona to the driver. "I know we're being atrocious, you're being so sweet." She brushed the back of the driver's leather jacket with her knuckles. He was smiling with terror. The cab swung hard around; Lionel was pushed against Leona.

"G-force," he said. "I'm a G-man."

"I am a pathological fabuphobic."

"You are not," said Lionel.

"Oh, do I so want those crab balls? I can't wait."

"They are the most lovely food," said Leona, "ever created in history."

"Is it expensive?" said Lionel.

"It's super not. It's like free. Is it not free, sweetie?"

"It's almost free. Lionel, can I use your phone?"

Lionel watched the street flash by; other cars were missing them like asteroids. His teeth were numb.

"Timmy," Katrina was saying into his phone, "call me, sweetness. Lionel, what's the number?"

He didn't know how he had ended up with the fun girls. He had thought he would have one drink at this stupid gallery opening and then he had been in the washroom with Katrina and now his teeth were numb and they were on their way to spending a billion dollars; they were on their way to spending the kind of money that you would need an act of parliament to approve. You couldn't phone up the fun girls and get them to come out with you; if you wanted them to come to a party they were too exhausted, they talked of staying home with gay friends and watching sitcoms. You never knew where they were going to be, you had to just be in their path. Sometimes they decided to take you with them and sometimes they didn't. If they swept you up along, it was on their terms.

He swallowed the nasty taste. Now his throat was closing up and he began to feel the acceleration of time or whatever it is that happens, that high whine of the turbocharger kicking in, the sense that the DJ has upped the pace of the beat. Bright cars were hurtling past. It was unclear how the driver, a tiny, dark, shrunken man, was navigating between them, but they were safe from death with him.

Katrina pulled her leg in and draped it over Lionel's thigh. He wanted to touch the textured pantyhose on her knee, but didn't.

When they had surrounded him at the gallery—not a gallery, really, a warehouse with its walls quickly painted white and the hangar door pulled up so the cold air filled it—he had had the feeling you got when the older girls in school decided to play with you for fun (even though Lionel was ten years older than these women, he still felt younger): they tell you you're so cute and then laugh. It was as if they were ruffling his hair.

Once, a year before, in some restaurant, he had expressed mild reservations to Leona when she had kissed him rather firmly on the lips in front of Treena (when he had been seeing Treena) and Leona had said, suddenly cold, "Honey, tell her to relax, why would I come on to you when I have *that*?" and pointed to Marco, her club-owning boyfriend, which had made Lionel sink and feel old.

In the bathroom at the gallery, Katrina had been quite businesslike too. She made him check his nose in the mirror and sent him out again.

It was after, by the bar, that they had had their who-can-kiss-Lionel-the-best contest. A lot of people had looked at that.

Only Katrina and Jennifer had actually played that game, but played quite hard at it. Lionel could tell that Leona did not want to play, which was disappointing again.

The cab stopped outside a corner restaurant in a basement that glowed orange. The women spilled out. Katrina murmured to Lionel through the window, "Tip him a lot," and then said to the driver, "You're so sweet, were we too terrible?"

They went down the stairs to the restaurant and Lionel paid the cab and followed them. The driver winked at him and drove off manically.

Sweet was all red. Six months before that, all restaurants had been white, like airports. Now all restaurants were red or orange or amber. Lionel thought that this particular place had once been white, even quite recently, but he wasn't sure if he had been here.

They sat in a circular booth and the tattooed cowgirl waitress gave them menus, and then Leona and Katrina told her that her boots were wonderful and her hair was wonderful and they just loved all of her and did she have those crab balls; they all ordered vodka drinks.

"Look," said Katrina, holding the menu, "what did I tell you, is this not like free? It's free."

Jennifer leaned towards Lionel and murmured, "I don't have any money."

Then Katrina and Leona took off to the washroom again, while Jennifer called someone named Timmy on Lionel's cellphone and left Lionel's number with him, and then everyone was back and they all rubbed up against Lionel and talked about kissing again.

"Look," said Lionel, "there's Amanda and Ian, they were at the gallery. Actually there are a lot of the same people here."

"Let's ignore them," said Leona.

"I did a radio doc with him once," said Lionel, "with Ian. I bet he wonders what I'm doing here."

"We should kiss you in front of him," said Katrina.

"Okay," said Lionel. "Who's first."

Jennifer leaned over and kissed him quickly on the lips.

"Come on," said Lionel. "Really. I'll show you how to kiss."

"All right. Really?"

"Sure."

Katrina and Leona leaned forward with interest.

"We're really going to do this, though."

"Yes." Lionel put his hand behind her neck and drew her head to him. He wet his lips, then brushed them against hers, then closed his eyes and opened his mouth against hers. He played with her tongue as best he could. He was just starting to relax into it when she pulled away.

"All right," said Jennifer, "you've made your point." She got up to go to the washroom. She asked for Leona's purse to take with her.

Leona and Katrina were whispering something together and Lionel asked them what it was. They didn't answer.

"It's not so much the size," Katrina was saying, "it's the fit. It's when it's like a beautiful boot that really fits you."

"Although let's not kid ourselves," said Leona, smoking, "size does matter."

"Absolutely."

"Marco almost hurts. All the time."

Lionel decided he didn't want to hear any more of this conversation. He watched the cowgirl approach them and was taken with her belly piercing, which was exactly the same little snake as Treena's had been. Jennifer was also back and watching Lionel stare at the waitress.

They ordered seven plates of food. Lionel gave the girl his credit card and watched her swing away.

Katrina said, "She's cute."

Jennifer said, "In a kind of stripper way, a kind of child-bride stripper way. Lionel likes that."

"Can we smoke here?"

"Sweetie, we can do anything we want."

"Is that Ian the one you heard that thing about?"

"What thing? Oh that."

"What thing?"

"Huge."

"What? Him? He is?"

"Like unnatural. A firehose."

"Like some kind of deformity."

"A cripple."

"Lionel, what's the matter? You look like you're going to cry."

"We boring you, Lionel? Or are you going to throw up?"

Lionel was carefully staring out at the crowd at the bar, which now included Ian and Amanda and Anita Wheelright and Anuparna Dutta, from the previous party. They kept glancing over and looking away again as if embarrassed, or at least that was how it seemed to Lionel.

"Lionel is angry because of that thing I said about strippers, because he's thinking of his little child-bride, which is sweet."

Lionel was trying not to feel sick. He didn't know how Jennifer knew about the stripping. He supposed, then, that everyone knew. He squeezed his hands into balls and stared doggedly at Anuparna Dutta.

"Don't be upset, Lionel, it was a silly thing to say, I didn't mean anything. I think she's quite sweet. And it's so sweet that you're so stricken, you're like a little puppy." Jennifer leaned over and kissed him on the cheek, and so did Leona and Katrina.

It was impossible for Jennifer to know, even if she did know about the strip club and the lap dancing and who knew what else, how much pain it caused him to even remember it for one second. So he had to concentrate now on not feeling bereft, which was a difficult thing to do. It had started with the waitress and now was like a gas in the air.

The seven courses arrived and everybody enthusiastically tasted one thing and left the rest. Lionel tried a satay skewer but could not finish it. The piles of noodles looked like snakes and insects, so no one touched them. There were four crab balls, which got eaten, so they ordered another plate of them.

"That was absolutely the most delicious thing ever produced in the history of humanity."

"I'm not hungry anymore."

"And it was *so free!* Was it not free?"

"I need to smoke *so* much more."

"I need to smoke my head off. I need to smoke the fuck out of myself."

"I'm just asking, was that not the best thing?"

"Where are we going?"

"Did Timmy get back to you?"

"Is there anyone else we can call?"

"I better call Marco."

After Lionel paid, he found them on the sidewalk outside. Katrina was talking on his cellphone. Leona had to go home to Marco. Katrina had to go to a thing for breast cancer. Jennifer said, "We'll go to my house," and put her arm in Lionel's.

"I have to crash," said Lionel.

"Bye love, sweetie, you're wonderful."

"Oh," said Katrina, leaning out of a cab window, "your phone." She tossed it to him.

"No you don't," said Jennifer, "I have goodies."

"Oh. What kind?"

"Wait till you get there." She had stepped into the street and was hailing a cab.

"Can you relax me?"

"Yes."

"Okay." He opened the cab door for her.

Jennifer lived in a condo that was all open except for a sleeping loft. There were books everywhere, and neat stacks of students' essays. Her computer was on, a lamp burning next to it, an art-history book open under the light, her reading glasses folded on the text. Her computer screen spun three-dimensional silver words. If you looked closely you could read them: *I'm stupid, I'm smarting.* The glasses sitting in the lamplight made Lionel feel strange: They reminded him of Jennifer's other self, which was considerably more frightening than her fun girl self, and he was not sure he wanted to be here for it. He wondered what it would have been like to have her as a professor, or a T.A., which was more accurate in her case, and whether he would have lusted after her.

He sat in a leather chair and she brought him straight vodka on ice, and another glass of water, and she kicked off her pointy, feline boots and curled her legs up on the sofa and lit a cigarette and threw her hair back. She pulled on the cigarette and let it out in a vertical jet, her eyes closed. It looked like the most pleasurable thing anyone had ever felt.

"You choose the music."

He got up, sluicing the burnt taste of vodka through his teeth, and scanned the CD rack. It was all full of female singers. He walked along a bookshelf, looking for fiction. There was quite a lot of fiction, surprisingly, and not all of it, not even mostly, by Sylvia Plath types. He was pleased. "Have you read this? This Updike?"

Jennifer was kneeling on the floor now, opening a plastic pouch and shaking the powder onto the glass of the coffee table. She shook two orange pills out from a plastic prescription bottle, and they bounced and spun.

"What are we having?" said Lionel, turning back to the bookshelf. It seemed as if he shouldn't watch, as if it was impolite.

"Flesh."

"Is that that upper-downer thing?" He couldn't not watch.

"It's just Xanax. It's best of all with Clonazepam, but I'm out. I call it Flesh because. . ." She licked a finger and picked up some residue with it. She rubbed it onto her gums. She leaned over to her purse and pulled out her wallet. "Because the Xanax is orange, and you mix it with the blow and it goes a lovely flesh colour. And because. . ." She pulled a credit card from her wallet and crushed the pills against the glass. "It makes you feel all touchy. Like you want to touch flesh." She scraped the pill powder into a pile. Then she pushed the pile of coke into it. "Eros," she said. She mixed the orange powder into the coke. "Thanatos."

"All right." Lionel yawned. "Hey! I can't believe this! You have Firbank! What the hell do you have this for?"

"Someone gave it to me."

"Have you read it? Oh, you must. You absolutely must." He pulled it down from the shelf. "Once you start, you'll see. You absolutely cannot stop."

He opened it and sat on the couch behind her, his knees against her back. She rolled up a bill, leaned, and snorted two lines. "Listen. Listen to this. *Looking gloriously bored, Miss Miami Mouth gaped up into the boughs of a giant silk cotton-tree. In the lethargic noontide—*"

"Here."

Lionel kneeled by the table and took the bill. "Ow. It burns"

"A little."

They both sat on the sofa, sniffing and wiping their noses. Jennifer pulled her knees up again and leaned her head on his shoulder. He picked up the book. "There's some really wicked dialogue. Let me find this—"

"Let me read this first page."

"Hang on. After I go. I just want to find this."

She pulled the book from his hands and read, frowning.

He sneezed.

Then he rolled his head onto the back of the sofa and looked at the ceiling. There were circles of orange lamplight on it. The apartment seemed deadly quiet as she read.

He slipped off the sofa and went to the stereo. He found some Bach violin and put it on.

When he sat with her again, he saw that she had put the book down on the coffee table without marking the page.

"Did you like it?"

"Yes. It's funny." She said this without colour.

Lionel rested his head again and let the music thread its way into him. The circles of lamplight on the ceiling were still. The corners of the walls were sharp lines. The violin overlaid them as if by pattern. They fit together. He said, "Did you know that Bach had twenty children?"

"Yes, Dad."

"By two wives."

"Yes."

"Oh. I find that extraordinary."

"That I know that?"

"No, no. Having twenty children. One thinks of composers as intellectuals, and one hardly expects . . ." He sighed. It was not important to finish that, although it was interesting. He felt the calm washing his veins. And yet the lines were so sharp.

After a time he said, "This is the most extraordinary feeling."

"Yup."

Then they were still again for some minutes. He felt as if he had never heard this music before, never known anything beautiful. He didn't feel sleepy, he didn't feel edgy. He was listening to the music and wide awake. "Three of his sons became composers," he said quietly, "and well-known. It is extraordinary. Out of sixty Bachs we know by name, something like fifty-three were musicians."

She sighed. He sipped his vodka, which tasted like cold water.

He picked up the book again and said, "Let me find this one piece of dialogue."

She put one hand, flat, over the page. "I don't like being read to. I want to read it myself."

"But you'll like it. I'm good at it. I do the voices and everything." He didn't know why he wanted to do this so much.

She sat up. "All right, Lionel, why don't you read it to me, why don't you read everything to me. Show me, Lionel, I don't know anything, explain the world to me. Isn't that what you got to do with Trixie or Misty or whatever her name is?"

He put the book down and stood up. He walked quickly to the washroom.

When he came out, she said, "I was just joking, you know."

"I'd better go."

"Are you crying?"

He went to the closet near the door and looked for his coat. She followed him, slipping in her stockings.

"You are. You are crying."

"Treena," he said. "Her name is Treena."

"I knew you were. Sit down for one second."

She took him by the hand and led him back to the sofa, where he sat dumbly, with his coat on.

"It was just a joke," she said.

"You know what?" he said quickly. "You know what's really a joke is that you're right. You're absolutely right, that is exactly what I want, to know everything and explain everything, and for you to listen, and that's exactly what I had with Treena, and she did listen and she wanted to hear everything I had to say, and you can laugh, but it was really wonderful."

"Wow," she said. "That's bad."

"No, it's not. It's lovely."

"Okay. Whatever. I guess I understand that."

He shrugged. It was hot in his coat but he couldn't stand. Nor could he take his coat off. The music was weeping, it was devastating.

She said, "It's a little bit sick, isn't it?"

"No."

"Why don't you just get a pet?"

"That's funny."

"Take your coat off."

"I have to go." He stood up. "I guess I do have this thing about being either a teacher or a student. I always have to be one or the other. I've talked to my shrink about this. I—my dad was a teacher. So I want to be one all the time. I find it kind of romantic, I guess."

She said very gently, "Right. But you forget that I am a teacher. And you can never explain the world to me. And I don't want to be your teacher or your student."

"Yeah." He stood up. "Thanks for the blow. And stuff."

He walked to King Street for a cab. The temperature had dropped; he had to button his coat. His cellphone rang. A hoarse voice said, "Katrina."

"Oh. No. Sorry, she's gone."

"Who's this?"

"This is Lionel. It's my phone."

"Katrina wanted me," said the guy.

"Yes. She called you from my phone. But she went home. Who is this?"

The line was dead.

There were no cabs on this deserted end of King where the condos began. Lionel began to walk east, back towards Bathurst. He wondered what he would do when he got to his dark apartment, as he probably couldn't sleep. Now would be a good time, actually, to have a dog, a dog that would be happy to see him, movement in the apartment, and he would have to take him out for a walk in the cold.

It wasn't really the absence of Treena that was bothering him, or the vanishing of Treena, the fear over what had happened to Treena that had been cutting him for the past four months; that had faded, really, over the last few weeks. He was okay with that now, not reeling with panic every time he saw a pornographic magazine on a corner-store shelf, not calling the last number he had for her every week. He was not writing letters to her on his computer any more.

He knew what it was that was bothering him, and it was something that he did not want to think about or even admit, because it had not bothered him for some five years, and should no longer bother him.

A cab almost killed him when he raised his hand at it near Bathurst. Once he was inside it and racing again through danger, again miraculously avoiding death as if suspended in a protective bubble, his phone rang again.

"Hello?"

"Who's this?"

"Well now," said Lionel, listless, "you called me, so why don't you tell me who you are?"

"It's Timmy, bud. Where's Leona?" There was a loud noise behind Timmy's voice, shouting, and a beat.

"Ah. Timmy, Leona went home. This is Lionel."

"Lionel? You a friend of Leona?"

"Yes. She used—"

"So where is she?"

"Timmy, sir, she went home."

"Listen, I don't have a lot of time, all right? I'm on Yonge Street. Where are you?"

"Timmy," said Lionel, "Timmy, honestly, Leona's not here."

"Don't jerk me around here, all right? Where is she?"

Lionel shut off his phone. They were approaching his corner. He had to get off at an alleyway because he could only get into his apartment by a rear fire escape. Once he was up the fire escape and had wrestled with the lock that stuck, his phone rang again.

The green screen said Private Number. He switched off its power. He took off his coat and turned on as many lights as he could and turned the heat up and put music on the laptop, queued three full-length concerts that would last him all night, and turned it up loud (the first was Schumann piano, mad and jangling, which his father had loved), and poured some Scotch and paced, wondering why he was thinking of his father now, his father whom he so wanted to be like, and whom he couldn't call now, much as he wanted to, because he was dead.

GENTRIFICATION

I T WAS, if anything, getting worse, the intersection. There was a new girl staggering around in broken heels and a miniskirt. She came rushing and tripping out of the doughnut shop into the cluster of guys in black hoods on the sidewalk, shoved her way through them and started yelling at someone farther off, walking fast in that jerky and deliberate way Tracy had come to recognize. She came right towards him, glancing at him quickly, in a mesh shirt over a black bra, and the black bra was loose and had slipped down below her nipples, which were thrust through the mesh. And her skinny legs were bruised and scabbed. There was no way to tell, with these women, how old they were: from far they looked like teenagers because they were so thin, but up close they could have been between twenty-five and fifty. They were sometimes missing teeth.

Tracy walked on, the pink nipples in the fall air flashing on his retinas like the imprint of a bright light.

There was no denying it: it was getting worse. Yesterday he had seen a black SUV cut off another black SUV right in the middle of the main street, and two white guys in black jackets had got out and flashed badges and pulled out the two guys in the other car, and those two guys looked exactly the same as the first two, except they weren't cops. And they were spreadeagled and searched against the car hood, just like on TV. Nobody passing had stopped to look. Everyone just kept their heads down.

He had seen that same girl the week before riding a child's tiny bicycle. In her heels. As if there was somewhere she really had to go. And Morgan had had her bicycle stolen from the back garden just the week before. They were, he and Morgan, both looking at every rack of bicycles they passed now, in case hers showed up. They knew it couldn't have been taken far.

But it was still only the big intersection that was bad, really: their little street was quiet, during the day at least, and their little house right down at the end, at least two hundred yards from the main street, and you didn't have to walk far along that bad street before you could get on a streetcar. It was only Morgan who had to do that anyway; Tracy himself walked in the other direction to get to his train, down through the old factories to the commuter line, and that area was almost totally transformed, all animation studios and loft sales offices. That would no doubt come, soon enough, to them, just a few blocks over. He was still sure they had made the right decision.

But there right in front of him was a group of people of all ages, walking towards him, and he knew right away what they were: there were the three bald young guys in track suits, and the grandmother pushing the baby carriage, and two other kids dancing around, and the vast shopping bags from the dollar store, and the language you couldn't identify—at first he had thought Slavic, then Arabic, and it was none of these. They passed him noisily; they hadn't been aggressive to him yet, even when the bald guys were in their packs without the women. They seemed happy to be there so far. They had all come before they changed the refugee status thing coming from the Czech Republic. There would probably be no more coming. Already they had their community organization and were taping up posters in their fantastic language, with lots of k's and i's, a language for warfare, and all the posters had the word ROMA at the bottom, sometimes with an exclamation mark, like a soccer chant.

He rounded the corner, and heard yelling, the same old guy, Leslie, if that was his name, it was something androgynous, like Tracy's own name, so it was something he was sensitive to, although god knows why he could never remember if this old guy was Leslie or Francis, it was something like that, god knows he had heard it five times on the day they'd moved in, and there he was, Leslie it was, on the square of concrete between the chain-link fence and the steps to the rooming-house, with his broom, sweeping up the broken glass that was always for some reason there, shouting happily to himself. "You tell me," he said very loudly and clearly, his head down, "you tell me if that's worth five grand. You tell me these fuckers aren't trying to rip the goddam shit out of you for five grand. My opinion, you want *my* opinion."

He always seemed absorbed in his monologue and yet he never failed to notice Tracy trying to slip by with his head down. "Good morning," bellowed Leslie or Francis, and Tracy called back heartily without stopping, almost at his own front door.

"Hope you got some sleep last night," shouted the old man, "you want to file a complaint I'm with you, you go right ahead, you got my support."

Tracy stopped, his hand already on the key in his pocket. "Something happen last night?"

The guy dropped his mouth open like a guy expressing shock in a cartoon. "Don't tell me you weren't up all night like everyone else with all that ruckus. Firetrucks here and the whole mess."

"Yeah," said Tracy. "Heard some yelling." He did want to know if the old guy knew who it was who had been fighting but then he didn't want the stories that would follow, so he just shook his head. "Just the usual, eh?"

"It's getting worse, you ask me," said Leslie, smacking glass into the concrete gutter around the house. "My opinion, you want my opinion, this whole thing's going to get a whole lot worse before it gets better."

Tracy shook his head, smiling, and shook out his key with a jingle.

"That's just one man's opinion."

"Got to rush," said Tracy.

"Hey now," said the old man, "let me ask you one question."

"Yup," said Tracy, on his own front step. Morgan wouldn't be home yet; he'd get an hour on the computer, maybe only forty-five.

"Answer me this: if a deaf kid signs swear words, does his mother wash his hands with soap?"

"Ha," said Tracy, "that's a good one." He failed to add, *Leslie*. He still wasn't convinced.

"Don't sweat the petty things and don't pet the sweaty things. Have a good one."

And there was the girl from underneath them, their tenant, shuffling up the basement stairs in her baseball hat and her dreadlocks, lighting a cigarette right under his nose.

"Hey Deiondre," he said, smiling determinedly.

"Hey," she said quietly. She did not smile. She was frowning. She loped off down the street, swinging her shoulders like an inmate in the exercise yard. She pulled her hood up over her hat. There was no way you wouldn't think she was a boy if you passed her.

At least it had not been her and Teelah fighting last night. And there had been no sound of the baby. There had only been a baby one night. It was quite possible it didn't belong to either of them.

The house was cold, which was good, actually, reassuring, it meant Morgan was finally listening to him about the absurd cost of heat in these old places, and also just the silly excess of it. He turned it up a bit, though.

From the bedroom window the street looked quite unthreatening again, if a little sad: the ranks of recycling bins in front of the apartment blocks had at least replaced the hillocks of green garbage bags and white grocery bags, and there were no new dumpings of furniture. Most of the tenants in the blocks were families; they didn't make trouble; and yet still every week there was a bed frame and a fractured dresser and a rug out there. Then they disappeared again; it wasn't clear if they were disposed of or picked over by others who had had their beds and dressers dropped into the street.

He had that knowledge again, rising in him like nausea: it was getting worse. He had been denying it to Morgan. But you had to face up to it. The Roma thing was good, really, he was happy for them, they probably really had been persecuted somewhere. They probably just wanted better dining room furniture. But two weeks before there had been a fight right on the main street, right in the middle of the intersection, not gypsies, two middle-aged white guys with shaved heads and stained coats grabbing, swinging away at each other, and then one head down on the asphalt and the other pounding. Cars had to stop in both directions. They were honking but nobody got out. The crowd outside the doughnut shop was watching and laughing.

And at night the girls came out with their bruised bare legs and their cigarettes. They always looked away when he passed them.

The computer was in what he was calling his little study, although officially they shared it, on the understanding that it would become a nursery. But he spent most of the time in there, on the computer; Morgan was starting to prefer the TV, in the evenings.

He did not check his own email; he had been doing that all day, at work. He went straight to AmateurEx where they had posted the photos of Morgan. The response at first had startled them both: three thousand views of one photo in the first twelve hours, three hundred thousand within a week. They had both thought, immediately, of money: if you could have a buck, or even a quarter, for each one of those views. If you had a gallery of a dozen photos, with a million views of each at a quarter a piece. It would take a couple of days of shooting, up in the upstairs bathroom with

the skylight. The variety would just come from the different pairs
of panties. He would enjoy buying them. But of course now she
wasn't interested any more.

There she was, still up, Samantha X—they had been joking, at
the time, about the cheeziest name they could invent, but now he
was a little proud of it—in the red panties and the white, one up
against a wall and the other on a white sheet, ass in the air, and
the full nude with a trimmed little thicket just artfully in shadow.
Her face was out of all of them, even her hair. The background was
carefully neutral, the one large mole on her thigh shopped out.
She had no tattoos anyway. Not even someone who had been in
their bathroom would recognize the beige tiles. They were just
beige tiles.

Eight new friend requests, just the usual pictures of cocks, and
the illiterate compliments. They were always half aggressive. And
one more couple, or at least someone posing as a couple, with a
picture of a naked pudgy lady in a kitchen in Belgium. She claimed
to be bisexual and find Samantha extremely beautiful and just her
sort. She was not unsexy, really, this pudgy lady in Belgium. Tracy
was already hard from this exchange.

He accepted all the new friends. The photo views were tailing
off; only three hundred more in the past week. They would have
to post more or they would fade into the archives; fans wanted
new poses. It was sad that they were going to lose this, but Morgan wasn't going to pose for any more. She had been flattered at
first by the attention but not aroused, as he had been, and now she
thought it was silly. And she didn't think there was any point as she
was not able to go to the gym nearly as often as before since her
courses, so she looked, so she said, completely different anyway.
There was no convincing her of the nonsense of this.

It was interesting that the most views were still going to the
white panty shot, not the full nude. Perhaps because there was the
slightest hint of a shadow at the crotch, the area that was intrigu-
ingly called the gusset, a smudge that could possibly have been a

stain of moisture. And perhaps the bathroom tile background suggested wetness or even some kind of unsanitary play. It was the least explicit shot but also possibly, in imagination, the dirtiest.

He had explained this to Morgan and she had wrinkled up her face and said "My God men are weird." It was after this that she had lost interest in the site, and in any new photos.

Tracy wrote flirtatious thanks to the guys who had sent their cocks to Samantha and promised more explicit pictures soon, possibly some that even fulfilled the unhygienic and clearly insane requests of bootlickr1968 and pissonmetx. He turned finally to the pages of some other amateurs, and hardened again at a few pictures of "nevadawife" in her kitchen, wearing a pair of rubber gloves. Her breasts were sagging and there was a bulge over her C-section scar, and yet both her nipples were pierced. There was a doll collection in a cabinet behind her, and a calendar on the wall with pictures of kittens.

He heard the front door snap and creak open, and he closed the browser. He stood at the top of the stairs and called cheerily down.

Morgan was already rattling around in the kitchen. He heard the clatter of the dishes he had left on the counter, and the distant beeps as she checked the messages he had already checked. He went down to her.

She hadn't taken off her jacket and was sliding in socks. Her cheeks were red. "No, I'm not okay," she said, "I'm not really."

Tracy coughed.

"I'm walking under the bridge, in the tunnel, after I get off the streetcar, and there is absolutely nowhere for anyone to move in there, with the construction, you just have to go with the crowd, and this woman, this thing, stops in front of me, turns around to face me, and she pulls down her pants, these like snowsuit pants, under this skirt, and she pisses, right there in front of me. She pisses." Morgan folded her arms and stared at Tracy.

"God." He put a hand in front of his face.

"It wasn't funny."

"It's awful."

"And she's blocking my way. I just have to stand there and wait until she finishes and pulls her pants up."

"Her snowpants."

"And she's staring me in the eye the whole time, like daring me to stop her."

"Huh," he said. "That's terrible. It's dark in there."

"I don't know, Tracy." She turned and began filling a kettle. "I don't know."

"You don't know what?"

Morgan put the kettle on the burner and the gas lighter clicked like an insect. "I'm starting to wonder. About bringing up a kid here."

Tracy sat at the dining room table, which was also the kitchen table and very close to where Morgan was standing. "I know," he said carefully. "I know. It's still pretty bad. But it is changing. It really is. Once they finish the construction on that bridge—"

"Did you want to make something?" She was looking in the fridge.

"I was going to do something with rice."

She closed the fridge and opened cupboards.

"Listen," he said, "I went by that place, Coral's or something, that place Stephane said was a lesbian bar, and it totally is, I thought it was, it totally might be. It's all stripped wood and, you know, an old jukebox. There's no sign outside. That's a sign if I've ever seen it."

Morgan was reading a box of couscous.

"On Saturday we're going to go for brunch at Valhalla. You're going to see beards. You are definitely going to see beards. You are going to see beards, glasses, you are going to see, I don't know, short-haired women. Seriously. I would bet—" He got up and stood behind her and put his hands on her pelvic bones. "I am not going to bet an eye or a testicle, I am going to bet like an elbow, that you are going to see one Swedish stroller."

Morgan stood still for one and a half seconds and then she put her hand on Tracy's, at her waist. She leant back into him a little. She said, "The ones that look like barbecues."

"With the baby way up high. The barbecue on wheels. The rolling barbecue."

"That costs two thousand dollars."

"With a little baby roasting inside. So you can watch it roast. As you push it."

She laughed.

He said, "Watch me cook."

At ten-thirty she was already in bed. She was reading a photocopied article and playing with her necklace. It flashed coral in the lamplight. He undressed beside her and she didn't look up. He inserted himself beside her. He said, "I should know. I know I should know, but where are we?"

"On the chart?" She turned the page. The title of the article had the words strategizing and acquisitions in it. "We're at seven or eight. Around there."

"And just remind me if that's good or."

She sighed a little. "It's at the end of the menstruation period, which I don't know, since I didn't bleed anyway, and the fertility period, so I don't know, it's on the boundary."

"Do we take your temperature?" He sat up.

"You don't do any fucking thing. Except put your cock in me." She didn't put the papers down. They were stapled together.

"No problem." He put a hand on her shoulder.

She held up one finger, and turned the last page. When she had finished reading, she folded the papers together. She put them on the edge of the bedside table and straightened them so that they were in line with the edge. Then she turned the lamp off.

She did not turn to him but lay flat on her back. He caressed her breasts and her belly.

He said, "Did you take your temperature anyway?"

"No."

"Do you want to do the mucus measurement thing?"

"Why? Just fuck me."

"Yup." He lay there for a second longer. Then he turned on his side and slid a hand between her legs. She parted them and he stroked her there. She became wet quickly and this aroused him and so he heaved himself on top of her. Her kissed her ardently and she kissed back a little bit and then turned her head away.

He bit her nipples as he thrust. She gasped and this encouraged him to reach down between their bodies and try to stimulate her, but she pushed his hand away. She bucked and ground into him, panting a bit, so he just fucked her harder. She pulled on his nipples. "Yes," she hissed. "I want it. Let it go."

A shout came from below them, from the heating ducts probably. He ignored it, feeling full and close, and then there was another, louder, and a thump. He slowed his rhythm.

Morgan went limp. Then they both went still and listened.

Even on the top floor, you could hear everything. You could hear them say hoochie and ho and bitch and cunt. You could hear thuds and crashes. Now Tracy and Morgan were lying on top of each other, their skin damp and cooling, and Tracy's penis shrinking inside her. They lay perfectly still and listened.

Every time this happened, Tracy dreaded hearing the wet sound of a smack. It would be something quite recognizable, probably, and if he did hear it, definitely and clearly, it would put him in a situation that would be morally difficult if not frightening. He did not want to have to deal with that. So now they were both listening for the sound of a smack.

"Shit," said Morgan.

Tracy rolled off her.

They were also both waiting for the sound of a baby, a baby they had never seen. And there it was, the hiccuping wail. It was as if it was coming from inside the walls of their own bedroom.

It made them both stiffen. Tracy put his arms over his head.

The baby cried and coughed as if it was choking, while the two girls in the basement shouted.

"Is that normal?" said Tracy.

Morgan hesitated. "Sure. It's just a baby. They sound like that."

The baby cried for another period which may have been only five minutes although it felt like fifteen.

"They're just ignoring it," said Tracy.

Then there was a real increase in rattling and screaming. There were shudderings in the walls that meant that something heavy had been thrown against them.

"Christ," said Tracy. "This is, we can't just listen to this."

Morgan sat up and pulled a pillow to her chest. "What are you going to do?"

"I'm going to have to go down there." He got up, his cock still waving around like a garden hose, and pulled on his bathrobe. Then he took it off and looked around for his pants. "I'm going to have to get fully fucking dressed."

She didn't stop him.

The basement apartment had a much-vaunted separate entrance, something that had allowed him to charge almost $900 a month for the two rooms, so he had to bring his keys and go outside in the cold, down the stairs into the little pit where the door was, a pit always full of wind-blown wrappers and cans and leaves, and pound on the door. He pounded and waited and pounded again. He felt a little queasy. He couldn't hear the shouting from out there. Perhaps they had stopped.

He was just turning around when the door opened. It was Deiondre, the one who looked like a boy, without her cap, fully dressed in her black jeans and hoodie. She said, "What?" Her little dreadlocks were wild and spiky.

"Hey," he said. "Everything all right in there?" He had rehearsed this.

"Yes. You got a problem?"

Tracy sighed. "Well yes I do, Deiondre. You guys are fighting all the time, and we can hear it, and it scares me, to tell you the truth."

"It's none of your business."

"Yes, it is, actually. It's so loud we can't sleep at night. It's a disturbance. And whose—"

Behind Deiondre came the other girl, Teelah, the girly one with the tight jeans. Her hair was straightened and tied back. She said, "What do you want?"

He said, "Are you okay?"

"What do you want?"

"I want to know if you are okay. I want to know if you are in any danger."

Deiondre snorted. Teelah didn't smile. She said, "Everything's fine. You leave us alone."

"No," he said, "I won't. You guys have to stop fighting. It's dangerous and it's, it's scary. It's my house and you're disturbing me and my wife and I won't put up with it anymore."

"Okay," said Teelah, "okay. Everything's fine. You leave us alone and stop bothering us."

"I will if you cut it out. And listen, there's a baby we can hear crying."

Neither of them responded. They were expressionless at this. This was an excellent technique, for Tracy didn't know where to go next. He said, "Neither of you mentioned there would be a baby moving in."

"What is your problem?" said Deiondre, and she leaned closer to him.

"You want to leave us alone now?" said Teelah. "You leave us alone. Everything's fine now. Leave us alone."

"It can't go on," said Justin. "Next time I call the cops." And he turned and leapt up his front stairs. He fumbled with the keys—because he had locked the front door out of instinct—and heard the basement door slam.

Morgan was up and waiting in the kitchen. "Whose baby is it?" she said.

"I can't ask them that. It's none of my business."

"What are you talking about? You're the landlord."

"And I can't kick them out for having a baby either. You know how that would look?"

"What are you mad at me for?"

Tracy put his head on his arms on the table. There was a silence in which they both listened as hard as they could. There was no noise. "I'm tired," he said, "of everyone being mad all the time."

She put her hand on his head, briefly, then disappeared up the stairs.

They had two couples for dinner, all university friends. Tracy worked all afternoon on a pure vegetable stew which was zesty if a little fibrous. One of the couples had a baby but didn't bring it because they had found a babysitter. Tracy watched them closely but they didn't seem any fatter or less happy. They seemed quite happy, in fact, and they both drank wine. Morgan drank a little too much wine.

Tracy was talking about the gypsies and he could tell it was irritating her for some reason. But he couldn't stop. He said, "But they won't stay here, you know. Right now everyone thinks it's going to be Roma central, this neighbourhood, like Chinatown or Little Italy, but it won't, because they're going to move on."

"Why?" said Priya.

"Because they're nomadic," said Dagmar.

"That's it," said Tracy. "They're essentially nomadic. That's how they've lived for thousands of—"

"But isn't it because of persecution," said Vanessa, "that they always move around? I mean, the Jews didn't exactly want to wander around the world for a thousand years either. And now that the Jews have found a safe place—"

"Not exactly a safe place," said Dagmar.

"Well, whatever, the point is their own place, and they're going to stay there."

Tracy was shaking his head. "But Roma though. I don't know." He didn't know why he wanted them to be essentially nomadic. Perhaps because it was more romantic.

"Are you saying it's in their blood," said Morgan, "in their genes to be nomads? Or have they just been nomads because no one's ever let them stay anywhere? Don't you think that's a little almost racist, like saying blacks have a natural sense of rhythm?"

Bang went the floorboards. A woman's voice under them yelled. It wasn't clear what she had yelled. Then there was a whole lot more thumping and screaming. Morgan got up and started pulling dishes off the table.

"Ey," said Tracy. "Not finished."

"Excellent stew," said Jordan.

"Is that your neighbours?" said Vanessa.

Morgan said loudly, "There's nut cake."

Something ceramic shattered below them, and then a chatter of the two girls yelling at once. It was frustratingly incomprehensible.

"Wow, that's loud," said Vanessa.

"Does that go on all the time?" said Priya.

"It'll stop in a minute," said Tracy.

And they all sat in silence to listen, staring at the tablecloth, except Morgan, who was clattering at the kitchen counter. And sure enough in a minute it stopped completely. And there was no baby crying this time.

"This one is not entirely vegan," called Morgan from the counter. "There's milk in it."

When he got off the commuter train from work, at the platform under the great humming freeway, Tracy liked to take his time walking home. There were a few blocks of factories before his street, and some of them were still functioning. There were loading docks with lights flashing green and red and engines belching as the trucks idled and grunted and edged angrily into the street. There weren't even any sidewalks there. There were warehouses with artists' studios lit up with fluorescents; you could see ladders inside and sleeping lofts and bicycles. And then half of them were under renovation, with sales offices for condos on the ground floor. No one ever seemed to be in them.

And then he would loop out to the main street, the big intersection where the McDonald's was and the streetcar stop. There was a row of bars, grocery stores of conflicting ethnicities—guy in skullcap and beard in one, Tibetan lady in another—and a barred-up pharmacy and a dollar store. According to the free weekly local paper, which held a great many graphic advertisements for prostitutes in its back pages, there was a massage parlour somewhere at this corner ("Sweet Aroma Therapy Centre all new girls real photo"), but he could not see any sign or marker, even when he stared at upper windows. You would have to call to get the address. It was probably up a dingy set of stairs and in a narrow apartment above a store. Tracy had never been to a place like this.

There were the usual bruised girls outside the McDonald's and he had to admit it was partly to look at them up close that he liked this detour. There were no nipples on display today, but one horrible stretch-marked exposed belly. Tracy took one more good look at all the upper windows before moving on. It would be possible that the girls in the putative massage parlour were the same sort of crack people, but more likely that they would be a little cleaner and more professional. He had heard that they were all Chinese. He had never had sex with a Chinese girl. perhaps they didn't even speak English, which would be troubling. They were probably all slave labourers, in debt to human traffickers, snakeheads, the people you heard about on radio documentaries, or maybe they were even Roma girls, with skinhead pimps. That would be a bad scene.

There was one of those Roma girls on the street right there, walking fast, in white jeans and glossy black hair. She looked totally clean. She avoided his gaze.

And now he was almost home and his stomach was queasy because, he realized, he was afraid of his house, afraid of running into his basement tenants. Which he really didn't have to be: it was his house, his own house, it was ridiculous.

At the top of the street, the old man, Leslie or Francis, out walking for a change. "Well now how are you doing yourself now?" he shouted.

"Just fine," said Tracy, risking, "Leslie."

From five yards away, the old guy asked. "Let me ask you something."

Tracy smiled but just slowed his walk, as if to show he hadn't time to stop.

"If you spin an oriental person in a circle three times." The guy stopped, puffing.

Tracy stopped too. "Yes."

"Does he become *disoriented*?"

The sky was the colour of a recycling bin. The street, at that moment, was ugly. Tracy squinted against the pale light. With effort, he said, "Ha. That's a good one. Another good one. I'll be seeing you."

"You take care now."

"Yup."

And as Tracy turned, the old guy said, "You want to do something about those two girls."

"Really." He stopped again. "What do you mean by that?"

"Those two coloured girls, I guess they're tenants of yours, they're getting out of hand. You let them fight like that you're going to have trouble."

"Are they bothering you in any way?"

"I'm just telling you it's not right. It's not right for the whole street. It's a bad example, and if they start—"

"What did you see? Have they done anything to you in particular?"

"Yesterday, the two of them fighting right in the street, up and down. Hair-pulling and cursing and the whole nine yards."

"Really. I'm sorry to hear that. But you let me know if they do anything to you in particular, all right?"

"If you have some reason, I understand if you have some reason of your own for not wanting to call the cops on them, that's fine, in this neighbourhood it's none of my—"

"Listen," said Tracy, "don't you worry about anything. I will—"

"I'm just saying, if you want some help, and no trouble with the cops, you just talk to me, I've been in this—"

"Thanks Leslie," said Tracy, "I've got it under control. I've got to go."

"Francis," said the old guy, "Francis Doyle."

"Sorry. Francis."

"You have yourself a good one," said Francis, *Francis Doyle*. "You got to wonder one thing, though."

"What's that, Francis."

"You ever wonder, what was the best thing before sliced bread?"

"Okay. I'll see you." Tracy walked towards his house.

Sitting on the bench outside the parkette was, honestly, a full gorilla suit, with head attached. It was deflated but propped up, perhaps by a stick, as if actually sitting on the bench. Tracy had no camera.

It was silly to be irritated by the old guy, *Francis Doyle*, and especially silly to feel humiliated by his advice, especially since the guy was probably a racist and had judged Deiondre and Teelah immediately. Who would say coloured these days unless they were being provocative. Or maybe he really was that old.

Deiondre was on her basement steps, in her hoodlum cap, smoking.

"Hey there," he said.

She nodded. She rubbed her face.

"You want to chat?" said Tracy.

"About what?"

"About the problems you guys are having."

"It's none of your business."

"I can't have you fighting like that anymore."

"Don't worry about it." She threw her cigarette down on his, Tracy's, unoccupied concrete parking pad and stepped on it with her giant high-top running shoe. "I'm going to be away for a few days anyway."

And at that moment a cab drew up and she ambled towards it. She got in it without saying anything more, and it drove away. She did not appear to be carrying a bag.

The most irritating thing about this really was that she was taking a cab, perhaps to a train or bus station, which Tracy himself would never have done. It wasn't the kind of thing one really should do, if one was living on welfare, which Tracy knew both she and Teelah were, because the damn cheques came to his own damn mailbox.

He opened the door to his cold house with some energy.

Morgan had a study group that evening. Tracy bought a veggie burger from the Vietnamese place and ate it in the cold kitchen. He wanted to play music loud, since he had the chance, but didn't want to seem hypocritical to the girls downstairs. But then one was apparently gone anyway. So he sat in silence and ate the veggie burger, which took some time as it was mainly grains and quite firm. It was at least a break from falafel.

Tracy liked to eat standing in the front window, partly because he sat all day but partly because he could see the street. He wondered if the gorilla suit had been taken away but couldn't see that far up. He could smell cigarettes: there below him, on his parking pad, was the other girl, Teelah, the one who actually dressed like a girl. She was wearing tight jeans that exposed a puffy brown belly, and a clingy white top under her bomber jacket. Her hair was straightened and tied back. She was pacing and talking on a cellphone.

He finished his burger as quickly as he could and tied up the garbage to have an excuse to go down there.

He greeted her cheerily and had to pass her to chuck the garbage in the bin. Then he sat on his front steps as if enjoying the unseasonably mild autumn evening. The girl ignored him until she finished her call. Then she folded her phone and lit another cigarette. She nodded at him.

He smiled. "Warm night."

"Yeah. Nice." She picked at her fingernails. "You spend a lot of time alone?"

"Huh?"

"I never see your wife. You seem to spend a lot of time alone. She away or something?"

"Oh no. She's here. All the time. Just not tonight. She works hard, at her courses. They meet for study groups in the evenings."

"She goes to school in the night?"

"Yeah, sometimes, sure."

"What she go to school for?"

"She's doing a Master's in Library and Information Science. She's studying to be a librarian."

"You go to school to be a librarian?"

"Yup."

"Tell people to be quiet all day."

"I guess so."

"I would hate that. I can't be quiet all day."

Tracy laughed. "Yeah, I wonder about that. About how she'll deal with it. She says she wants to."

"And what do you do?"

Tracy sighed. "I work for an environmental alliance. In Milton."

"Milton."

"I take the Go train."

"You saving the world for us, huh?"

"Yup." Then they both laughed.

Teelah shook her head again. "Well, that's the thing, she go away all evening, it's not good. For her to leave you alone a long time. A man gets into trouble." She had a little smile.

He laughed. "Oh I wouldn't worry. I'm not alone long enough to get into trouble."

"That's nice," she said. "A nice guy. A very nice guy. It's good to meet a nice guy."

"Huh." He couldn't make out her tone. She was still playing with her nails and smiling as if shy. "You ever go out with black girls?"

"Ha," said Tracy. She looked up at him with the same smile and looked away again. "Sure. I did, when I was single." This was not exactly true. But the point was he wasn't opposed to the idea.

"I'm not asking for me," said Teelah. "I'm asking for a friend of mine, she's single. She's looking for a white guy to go on some dates with. You know, someone who's generous."

"Someone to take care of her," said Tracy. He glanced at the girl's thighs now, solid and smooth in the tight jeans, with the enormous round butt popping out and a twist of thong rising above the hip.

"Yeah. Kind of. She has a kid so she needs a little help. You know a lot of guys, guys like you, that's what she's looking for. Maybe you could hook her up. You know anyone?"

"I don't think so," said Tracy. "Or, I mean, I'll certainly, I'll let you know."

"Or maybe you, you know you have so much time on your hands."

"Me." He smiled at Teelah, who smiled back broadly and then shook her head so her shiny ponytail flew. "This is your friend we're talking about, right?"

"My friend," she winked and giggled. She walked past him to her basement steps and held out her hand so her palm brushed his cheek as she passed by. "You think about it."

"Okay." She ducked into her dark doorway. "Thanks Teelah," he said without knowing why. He saw the thong from behind as she disappeared, a full triangle of black polyester, maybe silk.

He did not tell Morgan about this scene. She was back too late to talk anyway.

And the next day Tracy was off work, because they had rotating down days to prevent layoffs, and it was the middle of the week, which was always a little weird. He was putting on his running tights when the fighting started again; shrill shrieking this time. He could ignore this because he was going to be gone for at least an hour. If it was still going on when he came back he would call the cops.

He had his laces done up when he heard the screaming from the street. He looked out the bedroom window and there they were, right in the middle of the road. Deiondre had Teelah bent over; she was holding her by her hair and yanking her all over the asphalt. Teelah was flailing her arms, trying to hit, but Deiondre was keeping her just out of reach.

There was no one else on the street. Tracy was sure he wasn't the only one watching from a window. His stomach was cold, as if he might be sick.

Teelah got a slap in that made Deiondre's head jerk back; Tracy could hear its snap even on the second floor. Then the girls were silent as they struggled in earnest. Deiondre swung Teelah's head quite close to the asphalt.

Tracy knew he should not be hesitating, he should be running down there, running out into the road, yelling, as you would at a dog fight. It would not be difficult to break it up, once he got in between them. They were not big girls. They probably would not hit him. But he stood there. Someone else would surely intervene first. It was his silly running tights that embarrassed him most; he didn't want to go down there yelling like a tough guy on his spindly, shiny legs. This was terribly silly. If Morgan were there, she would be yelling at him to get down there right now. He felt sicker, amazed at this cowardice. He had not thought he was this sort of person.

He turned to the phone and dialled 911. He told them two girls, two women, were in the street fighting and someone was going to get hurt. He told them his name and address and they said they would send a car.

He went back to the window. The girls were apart now, hands on their knees, panting, staring at each other. Every few seconds Deiondre would bark something. Teelah was silent; she was the more exhausted. The street darkened with spots of rain.

Then Teelah just stood straight and walked back inside. Deiondre turned and walked up the street.

Tracy did not go running. He changed back into jeans, and put his hiking boots on in case he had to be authoritative with them, the cops.

The cops showed up in seven minutes. The street was empty and rainy. He watched their car pull up and just sit there. The cops just sat in it for a full five minutes. Perhaps they would just pull away again. That would be best.

Then they slowly got out the car, a burly guy and a burly woman, and they looked in their notebooks and then they lumbered over to his front door. His bell rang, and he heard the bell from the basement apartment ring too. He waited to see if the girls would come out first.

He stood behind a curtain and looked straight down where he could see the tops of the policemen's hats. They were standing in the pit of the staircase. He heard murmuring; Deiondre's voice. So at least she was talking to them.

This conversation went on for quite a few minutes but it seemed subdued. Then he heard the basement door slam, not too hard, just firmly. Then his own doorbell rang again.

He took a deep breath and went down.

The cops were identically square and ruddy. "Hello," said the male. "You make the call?"

"Yes I did." He didn't know if he should invite them in. He just stood there in the doorway.

"You want to tell us what you saw?"

He described the whole scene again, told them it was a regular problem, that he was concerned for their safety.

"Yeah," said the male, "thing is, everything seems quiet right now. We didn't see anything. They were calmed down."

"Did you see both of them? They both speak to you?"

"They both seemed fine."

The woman cop spoke. "There's nothing we can do if they're not fighting and they don't request our help."

"Okay," he said. "I understand."

After the cops left, he stood motionless on his staircase. It was utterly silent below. He knew they could hear every creak as he moved. He did not move.

He didn't tell Morgan about this incident either. And it was quiet that night; it wasn't until the next night that the music started, this time with no yelling, just a vibrating bass and thumping drum. They could even hear the rapper yelling over it, or whatever a Jamaican rapper was called. "Toasting, I think," said Tracy, washing dishes. "I think it's called toasting, that kind of chant. This is dancehall."

"Tell them to turn it off," said Morgan, from her books at the table.

"Yup." he took his time with the dishes. The music was horrible, really, it was angry and violent and it made the glasses on the shelf dance across the paper with humming noises. There was no way you could think with this noise. And imagine the ears of the baby down there, who was just screaming, screaming, screaming helplessly through it.

When the counters were dry he could put it off no longer. He put on his hiking boots and went down. he knocked on the door, and then he pounded. No one came. He tried this for a few minutes and then came back upstairs and called the cellphone number Deiondre had given him when she signed the lease. It rang and rang.

"This is it," said Morgan. "You're going to have to evict them."

"And how do I go about doing that?"

"Ask a lawyer. It's got to be simple."

"Yeah," came Deiondre's voice on the the phone. Now the music was tinny in his ear as well as thick underfoot.

"Hey Deiondre," said Tracy. "Could you turn the music down for me please? It's a little loud up here."

She was silent for a second. Then she said, "I'll try."

"You'll try? Deiondre, I'm asking you. Could you turn the music down. Please."

"We can't listen to any music now?" Her words were a little slurred.

"Of course you can. Just not that loud."

"We have a right to enjoy ourselves just like you. Even right here in Canada."

Tracy had no comeback to this. "Deiondre. Please. We can't hear ourselves talk up here."

She hung up the phone. The thumping continued unaltered.

"She hung up on you?" said Morgan. "She just hung up on you? That's it. That's got to be it. They're going. We're talking to a lawyer."

Tracy sat with her at the table. "Listen, they are obviously going through some horrible shit, I don't know what it is, but they've got no money, one of them is a single mom—"

"Tracy, they're violent and they're, they won't listen to you. They're rude. They're antisocial. I don't feel safe with them down there."

"I know. I know. But the baby thing really worries me. How do you evict an unemployed single mom with a baby? I don't feel, I don't feel . . . you know, they can get a lawyer too, you know."

"Oh, bullshit. Tracy, just stand up to them. Just do it. Or I will."

"Fine. You find the lawyer then. I'll pay."

"Just use the lawyer we used for the house, Fineman, whatever. All he does is real estate. It's one phone call."

"Yes." Tracy rubbed his eyes. He just wanted the music to stop and he would go on his computer. Actually he could just put on headphones and listen to his own music and it would solve the problem. He didn't know why Morgan couldn't do the same. "All right. Tomorrow. I'll call."

The music went off. Then there was some slamming and thumping, but no shouting.

He didn't call the lawyer the next day. He thought he would try talking to them one more time first. He went down in the evening, before Morgan got home, and knocked. The door was ajar; it just opened as he knocked. He stepped in and called hello.

He could tell from the echo of his voice the basement apartment was empty. It smelled bad, like a public washroom.

The fluorescent light was on in the kitchen area, bringing out all sorts of beige and grey stains on the walls and carpet. One of the kitchen cabinet doors was off its hinges and splintered. There was an ashtray and some empty Coke cans and nothing else.

He went into the empty bedroom. There was a garbage bag full of what looked like clothes. Hangers everywhere. It was here that it smelled the worst.

There was a dark stain on the carpet in the corner. He did not bend down over it to decide what it was. He switched off the lights and left.

That evening, Morgan was triumphant. "And of course they left just before the end of the month, perfect timing, so they got two whole free months off us. They knew what they were doing."

"I so don't care about the money," said Tracy. "I'm just so relieved we didn't have to go to a lawyer. It probably actually saved us money."

"And now they know exactly when we're home and when we're not. And so do all their friends."

"Oh come on," said Tracy. "They're not thieves."

"How do you know?"

"How do you know they are?"

She left the room. But she was only hanging her bicycle helmet up. She came back in with a hair elastic in her mouth. "I don't know," she hissed through her teeth. She was twisting her hair up. "I don't know any more."

Tracy began slicing an onion. He wasn't going to encourage this conversation. If he was silent they might just not have it.

"I mean," she said, "it's just intolerable. Isn't it?"

"What's intolerable? They've gone, right?"

"The whole situation. This whole place. Who do we get who'll rent that place who isn't like them?"

"Listen, we don't even need to rent it."

"What are you talking about?"

He turned on the gas. He poured his oil carefully. He took his time before he said, "This is what I've been thinking. We just turn it into a photo studio."

"A photo studio."

"Yeah. For us. It's great. It's got nothing in it. It's perfectly unrecognizable."

She stood as if she had to leave again. "Not that again."

"Well, it doesn't have to be just that. I'd love a space to work in. Just make myself a little more, you know, professional. Are you going somewhere?"

"I'm just getting the laundry."

"Well you get the laundry and we'll talk when you can sit down for two seconds."

She sat. She folded her legs under her on the sofa. "I thought we couldn't afford it."

"We'll figure something out. I was still hoping we could make some money off our photos."

"Off me."

He tried a smile. "Yes. You. Off you. Off beautiful you."

She turned and looked out the window. And then she sighed with what sounded like genuine sadness.

He slid his onions into the hot oil and the air filled with crackling.

In bed, later, she pulled him into her and he fucked her quite hard and fast, and she ended up coming, which she hadn't for a while. For some reason he didn't want to come inside her, and he just held out until she had finished and then rolled off her.

She held his hand. "What's wrong?"

"Nothing," he said. He was still breathing quite hard. "Just don't think I can. Maybe too tired."

"It's all the stress," she said.

"Yeah. No worries."

She let go of his hand and in a few minutes she was asleep.

He inched away from her on the mattress and took his cock in his hand. He was quickly engorged again and thinking of the black polyester thong, it probably wasn't silk, it was just sweaty polyester, rising from between the huge inflated buttocks of Teelah the black girl who had come on to him. He jerked swiftly, imagining her smell and her thick black nipples and spurted silently on his belly, gasping. Morgan didn't wake up.

When he took his walks he thought obscurely that he was doing research on the neighbourhood, perhaps in order to defend it better, and he had to defend it just because they had invested so much in it.

He walked some days all the way to where they herded the streetcars into yards and real railway tracks began, where there was a strip club in an old hotel beside a parking lot, called Exxotica or something as childish. He would walk past it and then turn around to come home and have to pass it again. Its doors were stainless steel and had no glass in them. He didn't know if the girls

in it would be white or black or Russian or Roma or what, because
he never saw a girl coming in or out.

And he still saw no sign of the massage parlours that were supposed to be at a couple of intersections. You would probably have
to call to get an address, which of course he wasn't going to do,
but he did just want to know where they were and how awful they
looked.

The sad hookers near his house were not Roma, they were
the ancient white poor who had been here since they had been
brought from, god, Ireland probably, a hundred years ago. Or they
had been small-town girls who had come here to be waitresses
and then got addicted, maybe.

The Roma girls did pass by occasionally, in their embroidered
jeans and their clippety-clop heels and their cigarettes and their
big sunglasses. The jeans were always a little too tight, the track
jackets synthetic, but their hair was so flowing and shiny, they
were actually, amusingly, sexy, he had to admit that. He was sure
they didn't have much money, they weren't the kind of people who
got jobs as real estate agents or cellphone salesmen, really—yes,
maybe they were genetically poor, what the hell, he would have
the courage to say this next time in front of Vanessa and Morgan—
but they still made themselves look hot with their pudgy little bellies and their supermarket clothes. And they liked being girls, too,
that was the thing, they were showoffs. If you came up to one and
offered to take her picture she'd probably leap at the chance, or at
least be flattered, if she didn't think you were weird.

But if you did it right, if you were very polite and professional—if you had a card, too, you'd need a card—and you offered
money, it probably wouldn't have to be a lot, because they weren't
real estate agents and for sure they needed money.

Because he was almost home and didn't want to be home yet,
he stopped outside the Blue Star Bar, with its scarred plexiglas
windows, a dim place he had only glimpsed inside. He saw that
there was a TV screen above the bar and a young Indian or Paki-

stani guy running it and no obvious drunks in the corners and he just stepped into it as quickly as he could, so he couldn't think about it.

It was too warm inside. There was one white guy at the bar and he had been drinking for the better part of his recent life. In the far corner, around a table, in darkness, was an entire Indian family: an ancient grandmother in a sari, a fat mother, a crawling kid and a baby in a stroller. They had shopping bags on the floor around them. They stared at Tracy when he came in but their expressions were neutral.

He stood at the bar and asked over it, "You open?"

"Sure, boss," said the young guy. He was pointing a remote at the TV on the wall, scrolling channels.

"Okay." Tracy sat on a stool. The family was still staring at him. Perhaps they were waiting for someone to come and pick them up. Or for this guy, the father, to finish his shift. Perhaps they spent every day like that watching the guy work. It was really too ghastly to be imagined, and Tracy was proud of himself for going in. And it would be rude to turn and leave now. "I'll have a Jack Daniels please, on ice."

The bartender said, as he reached for the bottle, "You want to make it a double? Three bucks more. Happy hour."

Tracy shrugged. "Why not."

This was a little silly at this hour, before dinner on a weekday, but this was his neighbourhood now. It was interesting to discover it.

As he sipped his large glass of whiskey, he saw through the murky window the gypsy girl he often saw outside the Hasty Mart, on a payphone (why were there still payphones? what was the advantage of a payphone?), because perhaps she bought her phone cards in the Hasty Mart and was calling the Czech Republic or Romania, who was not beautiful but who had such a lush little body she would, he knew, attract a great audience if anyone were to ever photograph it, her body, and it was something he thought she would not or should not be averse to considering, since it would be an easy thing for her to do and a small amount of money for him—what, exactly? maybe a hundred bucks a session, which would only take an hour or so, a hundred bucks an hour he could say—would probably be a lot to her.

The streetcar didn't come and the girl stood very patiently, just shifting her weight every few minutes from one leg to the other. If it had been Tracy waiting there he would have been pacing and cursing and making calls and debating the expense of a cab. But perhaps she had to get to a job cleaning buildings in the most distant suburb, the streetcar was just going to take her to the subway which would go to the end of the line and then another bus, and a cab was out of the question.

If he had a car he would offer her a lift. Of course he wouldn't, but maybe after another one of these dizzying vatfuls of whiskey he might be able to speak to her at least. He smiled to himself for even thinking of speaking to her.

"Nother one, boss?" said the kid.

Tracy made a show of looking at his watch but he was already nodding.

He supposed that it would be dangerous to get involved with a gypsy girl, in any way, as the men were quite possessive and violent. So it wouldn't be sex he was after, he would make that clear, if he did try to approach her; it would be a business proposition, a straightforward one.

She must have been furious and frustrated—it must have been ten minutes he had been watching her—but she didn't show it, didn't look at a watch or step into the street to stare down to its tunnel-like end.

By the time he had finished his second double and paid for it she was still waiting there, along with a half-dozen others, all equally patient.

He stepped into the cool light and his heart began to race with incipient cowardice. He stood on the sidewalk with them all and pretended to be waiting for the streetcar. He breathed evenly. He kept looking at the girl, and she did turn once and meet his eye. He smiled, and she did not smile back but nor did she frown; she stared at him for a second neutrally as if curious or at least evaluating.

He breathed. He would actually have to do this, and he could now, since the Blue Bird Bar—the street tilted a little bit every time he swivelled his head around. He was going to do something he had never done before and speak to her, just as he had never gone into a bar like that before, or, actually, been so wasted at five o'clock on a Tuesday.

And just as he realized this he saw, at the shimmering end of the street, the staring headlight of the streetcar, so it would be there in three minutes and she would be gone. He took a step towards her and smiled, nodded, and said, "Excuse me, hi. Sorry."

She took a step back.

"Sorry to bother you, my name's Tracy, I'm a photographer. I have a card here." He opened his wallet as if to look for a card. He riffled through it, frowning, as if he had a bunch there he just couldn't find, and he said, "I just wanted to ask you if you've done any modelling, and if you had an agent I could—"

She made a snorting sound, and her face was really something like snarl. She stepped back and held out a flat palm to him as if to fend him off. There was a grinding roar as the streetcar pulled up, and she marched towards it on her heels, shaking her head. The doors snapped open, and he held up his hands apologetically, like a soccer player denying a foul. He opened his mouth and closed it again.

As he walked towards home he tried to laugh about it. At least he had learned there was no talking to them. At least in person. But that didn't mean it was a completely dumb idea; it was all about the approach. You could, for example, put an ad on the internet, on one of those classified ad sites, and you could offer money and you'd have a ton of response.

If this was something Morgan wouldn't be interested in, and of course she wouldn't be, the whole thing would stress her out no matter how lucrative it was, it wouldn't be at all difficult to keep it separate from her. He could do it himself. He could have a separate cellphone that he would only have on during the day when she was at work, and it could be hidden the rest of the time. He'd need a private mailbox.

As he walked down his street he felt a lightness as he remembered the basement apartment was empty and there would be no screaming or confrontation, either with the black girls or with Morgan about them. You could paint that space clean white and hang a paper backdrop and get just a couple of lights. It was so small it would be easy to light. You'd only need space for one model at a time anyway.

He was even looking forward to passing Francis Doyle, out as usual in front of his steps, this time in a sweatshirt that looked as if someone had cleaned a soya sauce spill with it, and shorts, really, why shorts, just to show his veined legs and the grey socks?

"Good morning," yelled Francis Doyle.

"Good morning Francis," said Tracy, and then, quickly, "I have a question for you, Francis."

Francis Doyle's mouth was open. He nodded.

"Here's my question for you. You ready? My question is this: if a parsley farmer gets sued, can they garnish his wages?"

Francis Doyle stared at him. He adjusted his spectacles.

"Ha," said Tracy. "You have a good one." And he passed without further impedance.

Morgan was already home, early for once; she was on the computer but didn't seem too stressed; it wasn't even work she was doing, just chatting. She had a can of iced tea, which was an indulgence for her and a sign perhaps that she was feeling exuberant or at least in a good mood. The day was so warm she had the windows open. It was a pleasant place, their house.

He came behind her and kissed her on the back of the neck, and she turned to him with a little surprised smile.

"Hey," he said, "those paint factory lofts are finally on sale. I just walked past the office. There's a desk and a secretary. They've got models and mockups and everything. They look gorgeous. They've got those huge high factory ceilings, all that."

"Huh," she said. "We should go by and look. They probably have a model suite."

"Sure," he said. "For fun. I wouldn't want to live in a glass box. I love our little house." He stroked her shoulders, pulled her little ponytail out from under her collar. "But it's good for us. Really good for us."

"Huh." She turned back to her screen and he rubbed his knuckles in the back of her neck. She pushed back into his fingers, nuzzled his wrist a little with her chin.

"You know what else?" he said. "United Sulphates is finally completely closed. It's all over. I walked all around the plant and the parking lots. There's no trucks, nothing. And the buildings are empty. There aren't even the barrels in the yard any more. So that's a prime area for lofts. It's just a matter of time. You'll see the signs going up. They'll probably use the existing buildings."

"Sure," she said, "great, you could live in a chemical factory. Great for kids."

"People will. They will. You watch. Listen, once these things are all built our value is just going to shoot up. You know it is." Tracy looked past her head out the window at their little yard, and then over their fence at the garbage bins of the apartment block behind them. They were all overflowing, and some green bags had been piled around them. No one would collect those; they didn't take green bags any more. They would just sit there then, for a few months, until they had been dismantled by raccoons and squirrels and the sticky paper plates and sacks of diapers were just dispersed at the base of their fence.

But beyond that was the flowing main street with its hungry gypsy girls. Or whoever. He didn't even have to be limited to the neighbourhood, now that he had thought of advertising online. His audience was the whole sweaty internet. He would have to get a business name.

"You watch," he said, pulling at his wife's earlobes. "You wait. Once these things are built there's going to be a French immersion school right across the street."

"Mmm," she said. "Rub my neck again."

"Right across the fucking street." He kneaded her shoulders. "And a wine importer where the Hasty Mart is. You watch. Snobberton's or something."

She laughed.

"Before you know it. We're going to wake up tomorrow morning and Uvas Gomez is going to be a fucking design lab, with the Mies chairs and the Philippe Starck fucking eggcups."

"Oh yeah. The coffee tables made of Lego, no, made of CD covers. And the brushed steel toasters. For six hundred bucks."

"It's going to be called Silo. Or Casement."

"Encasement. Encasement Design Kitchen."

"Mailbox. Mailbox Collective."

They were laughing, and she was pushing her shoulders back against his hand like a cat. He stared at the blue recycling bins. You'd need a company name, yes, and an anonymous mailbox. There was a place you could rent them just across the tracks, by the commuter train stop. An ad on the internet. It was easy: anyone could put an ad on the internet. It was actually quite easy, now he had figured it out.

TXTS

A T FIRST he thought it was from Angelika. No one else would text him but Claude, and Claude had already sent him three messages that evening reminding him of insanely dull yet stressful tasks that were in no way urgent (*"did u contact claire m re liqor lic 4 watch event sept 7?"*) But Claude certainly wouldn't write *"how r u? will I c u tonite? X,"* which had just appeared on his screen.

There was a fractional pleasure, or at least a rush of blood to the diaphragm, on seeing it and anticipating Angelika's number attached to it, but he knew even before he scrolled up that it couldn't be from her. Indeed, the number was unfamiliar. He went through his address book, there at the bar, his thumbs blue over the screen, just to make sure, but the sequence was not part of his numerical universe; it might as well have been random numbers from space, like those signals you can pick up on short wave. He was the recipient of an erroneous flirtation. Or possibly nefarious spam, a robot hook jigging for live phone numbers in the wide sea of swirling digits.

Leo was hopeless at texting anyway; he resented it as the activity of junior people who had to spend their lives running around setting up meetings and deliveries like secretaries, jabbing their thumbs at plastic cases as switchboard operators used to plug and unplug jacks. He would turn his stupid thing off if he didn't think that Angelika might, for some reason, though it was unlikely, call. And ever since Claude's promotions manager had been away (Turks and Caicos or somewhere else she couldn't afford on what Claude paid her; Leo suspected a guy, a man, a lover), Claude had been simply dumping all the marketing work on Leo, casually instructing him to have five hundred flyers printed up or to pick five—no, ten—young entrepreneurs we could create an award for. Leo was a copywriter, a creative; it was a waste of his talent to spend his days, and now evenings, on the phone with the kind of twenty-seven-year-old woman who doled out freebies from beer companies and car rental firms. There were teams, armies, fleets of twenty-seven-year-old women across the city whose job it was to talk to each other about such things. And they knew how to text.

They were doing it now, all around him; there was white-yellow hair cascading all over the bar as the women frowned over their little glowing squares, or surreptitiously glanced at them at their waists as their consorts went on talking about cottages or highways. There were transmitters of various kinds lying on the marble, among the martini glasses and sticky flutes, black and silver, with little lights flashing, sometimes writhing in impatience. With his palms on the stone, he could sometimes feel the surreptitious vibrations coming right through it. It was this kind of bar. People wore ties in here, and they understood if you had to talk on the phone during your date. People here were busy people.

Leo's own date was apparently busy too, so busy that she had been unable to come. Or to phone or text him to tell him why.

He checked his stupid screen; nothing new. He read the wrong-number text again. *how r u? will I c u tonite? X.* He didn't delete it for some reason; it was nice to have such a message in one's phone. It was reassuring to know that such messages were being sent among people.

He gestured for another green martini.

There was a beep and then a flash: another one from Claude: *did u get answer re spa coupons?*

Leo deleted this one. It did not occur to Claude that Leo might be on a date at eight on a Friday evening, or rather this possibility did not strike Claude as a relevant fact, because Claude himself was likely on a date and texting angrily away as some leggy thing in a silk blouse pretended to read the bar menu. Claude did this. He would ask you a question and as you formulated a careful response he would pick up his phone and frown. And then, without saying anything, he would dial a number. Then he would hold up one finger. It could be interpreted as an apologetic gesture.

There was a tap on his shoulder, and Leo turned to see her, his date, who was older than twenty-seven but not much, and who was also blonde. She smiled brilliantly and held her arms out wide to embrace him. "Heeey!" she said, as if it was a great surprise to see him. "Am I late?"

They pushed some real estate lawyer sideways and she settled herself and they ordered her a green martini and she said, "Working late?"

"Oh," he said, "no." He picked the phone up off the marble. "But my boss would like me to. I'll put it away."

"He bugs you after hours?"

"Yeah." Leo glanced quickly at the screen before slipping it into his breast pocket. There was, unbelievably, another text message from someone. "How are you?" he said.

She was fine. She wore a black top that showed white cleavage, the perfectly shaped and smooth cleavage that had first sucked Leo's gaze into it the week before, when they had had to work on that underattended Scotch tasting. She was tightly built, tall and swanlike, and she curled herself onto a barstool and leaned to kiss him simultaneously.

Leo smiled at her, genuinely: at her breasts and her legs and her high heels. He exhaled a little tension. At least he could look at her all night.

She had powder on her face. She was younger than Angelika. She did PR like every woman in the world. She didn't mind the hard work; she got to work with some great people. She sometimes wondered that she got paid just to do so many great things and experience so many great products. And she admired some of their clients, she really did.

Leo listened and smiled with a rising dizziness. He wasn't sure, at first, if she was being serious, but it was increasingly clear that she was. He wasn't used to this. He hadn't been on a date in a while. He didn't know what to say. He knew it would be rude to bring out the big stupid blocky black phone and lay it there just so he could see it in case it buzzed, but he wanted to. He was curious about the last text. And then there was always the possibility that Angelika might call.

"I actually, believe it or not, admire Pepsi," she said, "I really do."

"Pepsi," he said. "Pepsi-Cola."

"Oh yeah. I'm a big fan."

"I can't really taste the difference," he said.

"No, I don't mean like what it tastes like. I don't drink anything like that. I just mean in terms of brand."

"You mean you admire their marketing?"

"Of course I do. Who doesn't? I mean, classic David and Goliath, right? I just admire what they did, what they've done to the field."

"Yes." He reached into his pocket. If he just pulled it out a bit he could glance at it and probably read the message or at least see who it was from.

"I mean like the whole points program idea, everyone gets that from the Pepsi Stuff campaign, and the interactive component of it. I learned a lot from that. We did a case study in school."

"Really?" He pulled out the phone, caught a quick glimpse. The first line of a text: *we culd hook up after the reception.*

"You ringing?" she said, and looked away. She drank her green drink.

"No, no, sorry," he said. "Didn't mean to be rude. Someone keeps texting me."

"Ah," she said. "Popular guy."

"Not really. It's someone I don't know."

She raised her eyebrows and smiled.

"You don't believe me?"

"Not really."

"Here." He pulled out the phone. He scrolled to the last message. "Here, read this. I don't know the number. Or anyone who sends messages like this."

"It's okay," she said.

"And now there's another one. Call me, he says, with exclamation marks. I think it's some guy texting his girlfriend. It's someone he knows pretty well."

"You can go ahead and answer it," she said. "Look, now I'm ringing too. Hello?" She slipped off her stool as she brought the blue glow to her face.

There were now three messages on his phone from the stranger. Laboriously, while his date chatted about her weekend plans to someone who was not there, Leo thumbed his way through the alphabet. He put some words together. *U R TEXTING THE WRONG NUMBER.* He hit send.

By the time they got seated in the dining room his jacket was vibrating again. "Christ," he said. "Sorry."

don't b like that, said his screen.

"So," said his date, "what do you like to do on weekends?"

Answering her as best he could—which was not well, for he could not really remember what he usually did on weekends, aside from this sort of thing—he wondered why on earth he had asked her out. He had not seen anything but the hips in their tight fabric, the swell of bust. He had liked that she drank Scotch and had a quick laugh. Surely she had said something amusing? He could not remember what it had been. Perhaps he had not spoken to her at all.

He thought she would be disappointed that he didn't suggest they stay out late together, or press to come in when he dropped her at her building, but she was quick and businesslike. She thanked him and kissed him on the cheek. He was relieved but also, he supposed, a little hurt. He was also, he had to be honest, a little disappointed himself that there were no more texts from strangers on his phone.

He went home and slept without pills.

It was carelessly, then, that he switched on the phone the next morning, in defiance of his own policy, before he was even dressed. It was Saturday; there was no reason to switch it on at all. He was yawning over his sink when he saw it sitting on the table, and he shuffled over with a glass pot of water in his hand and he just tapped the power button without thinking. He heard it tinkle to life as he was sluicing the water into the coffeemaker. He didn't think anything of his action until he was back at the table and there it was flashing demonically at him and making impatient music-box tunes.

It was that feeling you have in the split second after you burn yourself by grabbing a pot that's been sitting on a red burner: why the hell did I do that?

One from Claude, of course. *We need to chat today.* Instantly deleted.

Then the strange number again. It was a long one.

what happened to u? i waited for 60 mins and so did the others. It would nt have been difficult to tell me wher u were.

This one had been sent around midnight. There was another from an hour later:

I was embarrased, I told M and jen F u wuld b there. it shows a lack of respect that u told me u would show up and then left me waiting.

There was no message from his date, which was not surprising, of course, she wouldn't text him. She would email him, or not.

He sent a reply to the last anonymous message that said *STOP TEXTING ME I DON'T KNOW YOU.*

Now there was nothing to do except studiously ignore Claude until the late afternoon, just to make him wait. He should have set up a squash game. He turned off the phone and tried to read the paper.

His phone chimed mischievously.

New text message.

baby! u kill me!

Leo actually laughed at this. He put the phone aside.

But he couldn't read the paper. "All right," he said aloud.

He picked up the little metal brick and hit "reply." At length, he spelled out, *I'm sorry. I'll see you tonight.*

Then he erased the last sentence and wrote it as *i'll see u tonite.*

He sent it.

His phone was dumb for a while, to his slight annoyance.

He resisted calling or emailing Angelika all that day. He did not know how he filled the rest of it: he played squash with Stephane, he called his mother and she didn't need anything. He went grocery shopping. He filled his wine order from the Opimian, and still he went to the wine shop to see if there were any new Alicantes. He really did not need any more wine.

He watched a movie about fighting cars until about one o'clock and then slept without masturbating, in a kind of defeat.

He was in FutureShop. He was asking about the next step down from a digital SLR—not for him, he had one, a real one, but Angelika didn't really need one, she wasn't the type to really care what all the buttons were for, to adjust for a bright sky, to underexpose for mood, she wanted to take pictures of beautiful dinners people had made. She would use the flash. There was no reason, of course, to be buying a gift for Angelika at all. It might be an idea though—just out of the blue, no reason at all, not your birthday, nothing, just dropping it off for you, thinking of you. This was a really stupid idea and he knew it, he knew he wasn't even going to buy the stupid thing, but he was still going to stand here and wait for the eighteen-year-old clerk to come around to him because it was a way of thinking about Angelika.

And there was the foreign chime of the phone, that sound he still didn't recognize, the new text message chime. It was like the music behind the logo of a production company at the start of a film.

Jst wanted to say that was really nice. It was great to see you. im thinking of u. how is ur next weekedn?

It was from the same unknown number, except now of course it was known. It was a number he recognized as he would have recognized Claude's or Angelika's.

He didn't buy the camera. He went to a Starbucks and sat in the window and concentrated on typing with his thumbs. He would have to improve at this, understand the word recognition program that wanted to type "format" when you wanted to spell "ferret", or better yet buy a real thing with a full qwerty keyboard. Claude would be thrilled. Leo would then be one of those guys walking around with a full keyboard attached to his belt, some glorified delivery boy that people could reach twenty-four seven to ask him if he had had a chance to review the promotional materials and if he was available for a meeting Wednesday at eight.

He just used the old-fashioned alpha spelling, press seven twice for r, three times for s, get it wrong, back up, try again, do it in the wrong case, back up, try again. Whoever he was communicating with was much better and faster at this than he was, and so likely much younger. He didn't know if this person was male or female but it would be more interesting if she was female, so she was.

Eventually, he wrote a couple of long texts, as long as he was permitted, about how he was really sorry but he didn't want to see her, this person, any more. He found himself using Angelika's words, Angelika's words to him. He wrote that he needed some time to work things out, to work out his own needs, to think about where he was going in life. Time and space. And it wasn't fair, he wrote, it wasn't fair to her—it's not fair to you, he wrote, to go on like this, in this undecided state, because you are young, and I don't want to rob these years from you. You could be with someone who is much more certain, someone you deserve. Because you deserve someone who is totally committed.

On that note he concluded that they shouldn't see each other for a while and he wouldn't be answering any more texts. He hoped she understood and respected his choice. He sent it and looked around at the strange people in the Starbucks who were sitting there in their workout wear or fussing over babies in strollers and unaware of how strange things were in life.

Then he went home and sat at his computer and he wrote a friendly email to Angelika. He asked if she wanted to get together that week, perhaps after work some night, either Tuesday or Thursday, just for a drink, no big commitment. He kept rewriting it. Just a friendly drink. A drink as friends. He would like to be able to contact her and see her every once in a while. To see her as a friend, perhaps have dinner.

He sent this and then surfed listlessly for a while. He looked up the woman he had gone out with on Friday, as he hadn't heard from her. He saw with some surprise that she had some kind of blog. It was called Cosmo Girl. The pages were black with pink lettering. The subtitle was Adventures in Urban Dating—From A Single Gal Who Wonders Where All the Cary Grants Are? The entries went back a few months. She seemed to be going on two or three dates a week.

He of course scrolled to the most recent one. The entry was titled "Texting on the Job" and it described a date with a guy who had been taking text messages all through their date while trying to pretend he wasn't.

I could see him practically shivering with curiosity every time his little phone chimed. I could see him trying to keep his eyes focused on me—you know when you know when a guy is trying really hard not to stare at your boobs? It was like that but he was trying not to look at his phone to see who had messaged him. My boobs weren't even in it, I guess (although he didn't mind taking a good look at them when I arrived. I had deemed him worthy of my new Lejaby push-up from Under The Skin which, listen up ladies, is my new favourite emporium in the entire city). What's the etiquette on leaving the text message function on while you're trying to woo a lady? We should have some new word for that surreptitious glancing-at-your-phone thing—you know like when you want to glance at your watch in a meeting but you don't want anyone else to see you do it, so you move your hand to your lap and then you pretend to be scratching your wrist and then you quickly glance down as if you're looking for crumbs on your skirt? The Nod-and-Check, something like that. You clever ladies will be able to come up with something funnier than that—I leave it to you. Anyway, this poor guy was so eager to go check his messages he practically ran me through dinner. I hope whoever she was had just as nice a bra as I did—and that he got a chance to see it! Sonehow I don't think he did. Needless to say, this Mister Phone Romance won't be getting a second chance to show off his telephone etiquette with me.

Then there were a few comments from readers who had come up with cleverer names for him—Distracted Dater, the Light-brained Lothario, Text King, S-M-Escapade. But most just wanted to tell similar stories of assholes with digital devices.

He was surprised most of all by her energy—she hadn't seemed nearly as articulate over dinner.

He did get another text from the stranger, at about eleven the next morning. He was just coming out of a boring meeting that he hadn't needed to attend with Claude and the people from a leather goods store about the planning of a party involving a basketball star. The message said, *hope u feel as nice as i do.*

He didn't respond, although he felt like asking if sarcasm was involved.

The next one came just a few minutes later. *seriously, it was really nice to see u, and i am so glad you came over. i feel warm all over. we didn't talk about it, but i gues you changd ur mind about what u wrote yesterday in the pm. i'll forget it if u will.*

And it was right after his reading this that his phone rang, an old fashioned ring, there in the hallway on his way down to the coffee shop with an order for Claude and for Heidi the new office girl, a ring that said someone with a voice wanted to communicate with him. He answered as the elevator doors grinded open and he stepped away from them to go to the end of the hall to talk.

Of course it was Angelika, who had chosen this moment, right in the middle of the day and his office, to talk to him.

She was gentle but melancholic. She didn't think it was a good idea, much as she would love to see him and find out how he was doing, she just didn't think it was a good idea to see each other again. It was too soon. There really was no point, she said.

"No *point?*" he said, looking out over the white concrete city through the slit window at the end of the hall. The window was made of reinforced glass with a wire grid in it.

"Well," she said, "you know what I mean."

"No, I don't. What is the *point* of any social activity? Does it have to have a point?"

She sighed. "Leo, you've never got this. But arguing, or writing long letters, doesn't change anybody's feelings."

He went down to the coffee shop and sat in the window for a moment before ordering. He just stared at the street, which was busy and distracting because it reminded him of all the people in the world who weren't a part of the killingly, mutilatingly dull basketball and leather goods party that he had to go back and talk to Claude about.

He took out his phone and found the last text.

we didn't talk about it, but i gues you changd ur mind about what u wrote yesterday in the pm. i'll forget it if u will.

He wrote, *i'm glad we were able to work things out.*

The reply came back almost immediately. *i'm happy.*

Leo wrote, *so am i,* and on sending it he actually did feel a kind of pleasure, a warmth, the thing you feel when someone loves you and you can love them back unrestrainedly. He smiled at the street where people were walking in the white light to their strange jobs, all of them possibly having fictitious affairs with strangers on their cellphones.

He went to the counter where a new girl was working and he noticed she was pretty, unusually pretty, with loose shapeless clothes and glasses to try to hide it. He smiled at her and ordered his coffee and then, while he was waiting for it, said "You don't seem so busy today."

"Nope," she said. "That's one seventy-five." She wasn't smiling.

"Probably better for you when it's busy, I guess," said Leo. But she had turned and walked away.

CONFIDENCE

SHARON SAID, "It's really too bad we have to go out with any of them."

Jennifer was about to say something but took a drink instead. She squinted a little as she looked down the bar. Edward and Guntar and Ravi were there. Ravi had the best suit of them, and a finely checked shirt with a wide-spread collar, and he had not loosened his tie like the others. Jennifer did not like it when they loosened their ties. Ravi smiled at her. His skin was almost completely black against the pale blue shirt, and this was dramatic. Edward and Guntar saw him smiling, and they looked over at the women and nodded. Edward's face twitched a little as if he couldn't decide if it was cool to smile or not. They turned their backs. One of them said something and the others laughed loudly.

"Well," said Jennifer, "it's not as if we have any choice."

"No," said Sharon. She finished her wine and set it down on the marble.

Edward couldn't help turning to look at Jennifer again. Ravi saw him doing it and said, "So. Which one."

"Of those two?"

"Yes. Of those two."

Edward shrugged. He did not want to look shy in front of the
others. He waved at Chrissie for another beer.

"You know which one I want?" said Guntar. He was swaying a
little.

Edward and Ravi looked at him with interest.

"All of them."

They all barked a laugh like a shout. Edward felt immensely
relieved. "Fucking right," he said. "Fucking right."

Even Ravi had found this funny.

There were also Olivier and Charles Easton and that guy Bobby
who nobody seemed to know, sitting in the chairs around the
ottoman by the fireplace. Jennifer and Sharon had greeted them
when they came in and were looking at them occasionally. Jennifer and Sharon had not said this to each other, but they knew there
was always a possibility, if Edward and Ravi didn't come over to
talk to them, that they would end up sitting with Charles Easton.
Charles Easton seemed to be talking very intensely, and the other
two men were leaning forward to hear him in the thumping and
ticking of the horrible Italian house which everybody hated and
yet which Davey insisted on playing every single night of the
week.

Charles Easton was wearing a black velvet jacket and white
silk shirt, and he had a pocket square. It was preposterous, but it
really did look quite glamorous. And Olivier looked quite beautiful too. The guy Bobby had his hair cropped very short, in a kind
of menacing way. They all had their heads close together and were
frowning.

"I always wonder what they talk about," said Sharon. "I wonder
what Charles Easton is saying right now. But I never wonder that
about Edward. Or any bankers."

Jennifer squinted again. "Yeah. I guess. No. I don't. I never do."
She did a little yoga stretch with her back and neck. "You know, I

like this wine, but it's sticky or something. I would like to shift, I think, to gin and tonic."

Charles Easton was, in fact, at that very moment, saying this: "Then I chop a little cilantro, I pan-sear the scallops, and the secret is a drop of sesame oil right in the deep fryer."

None of them in the bar could see Lionel Baratelli, at this moment, because he was in the dining room with Jackie Farbstein. Jackie was buying him dinner. Jackie was talking to a girl on his phone and the waiter was standing there waiting for him to finish. Everybody waited for Jackie; it was a thing he could make people do. He said, "So, how was Thailand?" and he held up one finger to the waiter and he smiled at Lionel. "Did you lay waste to Thailand? I can't imagine Thailand surviving you in a bikini. You were the tsunami."

Lionel picked up the wine list.

Jackie said, "Whatever you want, bro, you choose. Four of you, in one villa? Was your sister there?"

"Maybe we need a second more," said Lionel.

The waiter went away and Lionel read the list as closely as he could, while Jackie Farbstein said, "You are dangerous. Dangerous. I'm not even sure I want to see you. So listen, I would love to chat but I'm just having dinner with my old friend Lionel Baratelli, the writer, you know Lionel, who is a wonderful and fantastic guy. And so I'd better rush, but I'd love to hook up later, if you guys know where you're going to . . . yeah, that's later, though. It's a tasting at nine, then a fashion show or something. So we won't make the tasting."

Lionel called the waiter over and ordered a fairly good Rioja Tempranillo, because it was not extravagant and yet something he would not have ordered had he been paying. When Jackie closed up his phone, Lionel told him what he had ordered and Jackie said, "Excellent, perfect. This is why I love you, bro. This is why we have to spend more time together. I need to learn these things from you."

There was a young man in the bar whom Lionel had noticed passing through. Lionel had seen him at this place, and at other places, several times before, and had been curious about him because the guy was always alone and he was always writing in a notebook, an expensive leather-bound one. The guy wore black and he had his hair slicked back like some kind of fascist poster and he always wrote with a fountain pen. Every time Lionel passed him the guy looked up and smiled. He made Lionel a little nervous, because he was obviously some sort of writer, and Lionel was pretty sure he knew everybody who wrote anything of any kind in this town, and particularly in this place. The guy's handwriting was vertical and regular, and it covered the pages in black, like a harsh and intricate tribal tattoo.

Sharon was saying to Jennifer, "I'm not afraid of shorting, margin selling, whatever. I mean I spent all that time in options, warrants, all kinds of derivatives. I'm not sure this guy knows who he's playing with. He told me he wanted in, I said okay, you know there's a five grand minimum investment, right? And I don't know if he hesitated for a second, just for a second, maybe it was my imagination, but he's like, Sure, certainly, no problem. I'm like all right.

"Yeah, that's his dad's firm, right? It's not really his own money he's playing with."

"I'm not really sure if it's an institutional investor he wants. I'm not really sure he's an institution."

"You don't need to waste your time with that," said Jennifer. "Stick with the big boys."

"I'll let my assistant help him." Sharon looked over at the guys at the end of the bar, at Edward and Guntar and Ravi, who were all red-faced now. "They are taking their time, aren't they." She undid the top button of her blouse.

Edward said to Guntar, "No no no no no, the XKR has the grilles in the hood. It's the little one. The XK8 is just a fucking boat. It's a fucking Taurus. The XKR is like a little shark. Three fifty horse."

Ravi said, "Three fifty what? It's the horsepower torque ratio you want to know about. Three fifty three fifty or three fifty three hundred or what?"

"It goes fast," said Edward. "I can tell you that."

"Stupid rims though," said Ravi.

"So," said Jackie Farbstein. "Lionel, it is so good to see you. I have to tell you, I have to tell you just one thing, before you tell me all about what you've been up to, which I am just dying to hear. I have to just tell you that it is just so great to be with you, I always enjoy seeing you, and it's just so refreshing, always."

"Me too," said Lionel. "I wanted to tell you about—"

"What was the wine you ordered?"

"A Spanish wine. It's sort of medium-priced, but I'd heard about it through this—"

"Excellent. Excellent. An inspired choice, as always, I'm sure. You had a chance to look at this?" Jackie unfolded his menu and stared around the room. "What do you think so far? Not bad for a Tuesday. That's usually the absolute worst here. And it's getting worse and worse. But it's not too bad today. You know those two at the bar? When we came in?"

"Yes," said Lionel. "Financial. And P.R. Run their own companies."

"Really?" said Jackie. "Interesting. You are so good at this, Lionel. You know this one behind you?"

Lionel twisted. Across the aisle was a booth, and in the booth was a blonde. She wore a black silk dress, which was a little unusual for a Tuesday in here. Beside her was a guy with a funny haircut, a big blonde guy in a sweatshirt with a T-shirt over it. He looked about forty, older than the girl, and he didn't look at all comfortable with his haircut. "Nope. Don't know the guy either."

"She's been giving me a lot of attention."

"She looks to be on a date."

Jackie was bent over the menu. "You want to try a little bit of everything?"

"Sure."

"Okay with you if I order? I haven't tried the new guy's stuff."

"Sure." Lionel folded up his menu. Now he wanted to look at the blonde who had been looking at Jackie. Maybe she knew who Jackie was. It was a little weird that Lionel rarely noticed any blondes looking at him, himself, Lionel, these days. And he wasn't any older than Jackie Farbstein. In fact, Jackie Farbstein was a couple of years older than he was.

"Shredded pork blinis with tamarind flowers looks kind of cool. What do you think a tamarind flower is?"

The waiter was there with the wine. He said, "Mr. Farbstein, Davey has just spoken to the chef, and he would love to suggest to you that they make up a tasting menu for you. It would be a five-course menu, and we could suggest—"

"Wow, you know, thanks, that is just a fantastic offer, and you know, I want you to tell Davey that we are honoured, that's a great idea, but I think I will take him up later on that, because I would really just like to try your regular menu for tonight. But if you have any suggestions of what you think is especially good tonight . . ."

"Of course."

"My friend will try the wine."

Lionel tasted it and then Jackie began ordering plates of things. He ordered enough for three dinners and said, "So. There is so much we have to catch up about. First of all, of course I want to hear about you and all your projects, and your love life, of course, which is always so fabulously complicated, but—"

"No, it's not," said Lionel, "not at the moment." He felt in his pocket for his phone.

"But first, I really have to tell you about this St. Tropez thing I have going, because I think you would be amazed, you really would, you'd be amazed by how fantastic it is. You absolutely have to, have to find some way to come over there and visit me, because we would have the most fantastic time there together. I have stories which would, well, you're going to hear them."

"Do you like the wine?"

"I love it, it's delicious, it's perfect. Cheers. Always great to see you. Anyway. I have this villa, I'm supposed to be sharing it with a guy I know from Miami, but he's never there. And basically I just chill, I hang out." Jackie paused, staring across the room. He smiled and raised his glass to the far wall. "I just got a smile out of her."

Lionel turned and sure enough, the blonde was raising her glass at them. Her date had his arm around her and was looking over a little dolefully.

"I think her date's a little confused," said Lionel.

"He doesn't have a chance with her."

"He has his arm around her. Hey, why didn't you let Davey give us the tasting menu?"

Jackie shrugged. "I like to control negotiations. It's my background." He looked at the blonde again. "That guy's a putz. He's out of his league."

"Negotiations?"

"Listen, this villa, last week, we had a bunch of people over, including this model who was. One second." He answered his phone. "Julia. Julia. Get out of here. Shut up. I can't believe this. How the fuck are you? What are you up to tonight?"

Lionel smiled at Jackie and pushed his chair back and Jackie gave him a thumbs up. Lionel walked first towards the washrooms but once he was out of sight of Jackie he wheeled around, through the private dining room, towards the front bar. He passed the young guy with the notebook open on his table. The guy didn't appear to have written any more hieroglyphics since the last time Lionel had passed. The guy smiled up at Lionel and Lionel smiled back. He was sure he didn't know the guy.

Lionel stopped to kiss Sharon and Jennifer, just as Edward and Guntar and Ravi were paddling down the bar to join them. Edward had a flushed and determined expression. His face seized up for a second as he saw Lionel step in, so Lionel stuck out his hand and grabbed him on the shoulder. "Hi," he said. "I'm Lionel."

"Hey, Lionel," said Edward. "Good to meet you."

"This is Edward, and Ravi and Guntar."

There were a lot of bone-cracking handshakes.

"Edward is a rising star lawyer."

"Not really."

"He's the youngest senior investment advisor at—"

"No no," said Edward. "Not yet. Almost."

"The youngest almost senior."

Ravi snorted. "I guess that makes me an almost senior too. And I'm not even a sleazy bond trader."

"Congratulations," said Lionel. He stepped out of their way so they could kiss Jennifer unimpeded.

Sharon said, "You want a drink?"

"No, thanks, I'm having dinner with Jackie Farbstein. I just came out to make a phone call. Listen, you know that guy who's sitting over there with a notebook? The guy in black? Who is that guy?"

"Oh," said Sharon, "That's Davey's cousin or something. He's the Northwood kid."

"Oh. William or something."

"I think. William or James. I think James. He says he's a writer."

"That's what I thought, because I always see him writing, but I know everyone who's a writer. What kind of writer?"

"He published a book of poetry. Or a play. I think. Yeah, it was a play. He's cute, too."

Lionel peered over at the kid, who was writing again. "A play. So how is he a member here?"

"Oh, you know they give memberships to artists. Free. It's a good idea."

"Yes, it is a good idea." Lionel took out his cellphone. "I had to pay for mine."

"Come by and have a drink with us afterwards."

"I will."

As Lionel left her, Guntar took her hand and kissed it, and she threw her hair back and shook it all over her shoulders.

Lionel went out to the lobby to call Sandra. She didn't answer, so he waited for her message and said, "So we've just sat down to eat, and it looks as if he's ordering everything on the menu, so we may be a while. I'll call if we go out afterwards. Maybe you want to come and join us." He was a little relieved that Sandra hadn't answered. She hated it when he came to this place.

Edward was saying to Sharon, "I mean I'm a little sick of Playa del Carmen itself, you know, like everybody, and Puerto Morelos too, I mean it's great the first time, like when you're in your twenties, but this place is inland, on lagoons."

"You are in your twenties," said Jennifer.

"Totally environmentally friendly," said Edward, "you get around on little electrical launches, totally silent, and there are five resorts total, and you can go to any of the facilities, spas restaurants, it's pretty—"

"How's the golf?" said Ravi.

"Amazing. Amazing. Greg Norman designed the course. He was there when we were there."

"A little hot, I guess, though," said Ravi.

"Did you watch him play?" said Guntar.

Jennifer and Sharon were listening and smiling. After a few minutes, Sharon caught Jennifer's eye and they both smiled even harder at each other. Sharon looked over at the table by the fireplace, where Charles Easton and Olivier and the new guy with the cropped head were laughing, laughing.

"My feet hurt," said Jennifer softly.

"We could sit over there," said Sharon in her ear.

"By this point he was like five under," Edward was saying, a little too loudly, "and we were just brutally hungover."

Jennifer leaned close to Sharon, and she knew it was rude and that everyone could see she was murmuring to her but at this point it didn't matter; she knew that the ruder she was to Edward the more desperate he would be to impress her. And Ravi she wasn't concerned with: she had already tried him; he was going to marry some cousin his family had set up for him when he was five. She said softly to Sharon, "Who's the new guy, Bobby?"

"Smart guy, apparently. Prof or something."

Jennifer sighed. "No, though. We always sit with clever boys. We can sit with clever boys any time we like."

Sharon sighed. She turned to Guntar and threw her hair back. She squinted her eyes at him and put her fingers at her throat to play with her necklace. "Guntar," she said, "do you play golf as well?"

What were they saying over there to make them look so happy and relaxed and interesting? In fact, Olivier had just said to Charles and the new guy Bobby, "I just said to him, you're wearing double-pleated pants, what are they, Dockers? Hello! There's a Guess store right across the street from your building. Three words: go in there."

That was what had made them laugh so hard, and this was why the women so longed to sit with them. But this is also why they knew it would be a waste of their time. They were not here for fun. They were here for the kind of guy who would find this conversation very gay.

And do you want to know what James or William, the guy in black, was writing in his notebook? This is all he had written all night:

Goldfish Club. Seven p.m. Raining outside. Trying to focus in the hubbub. The soul aches. Something beautiful about the way Chrissie pours the chardonnay. The wine like rain from her hand. The rain of wine. Sharon just arrived. Hasn't looked over here yet. Hope she doesn't sit next to me.

He had changed the name of the club, at least.

This piece was as yet untitled.

Jackie Farbstein was off the phone. He said, "So. Where was I."

"The villa."

"The villa. My friend. My friend. You have to come there. Okay, what is this now?"

"Rabbit dumplings," said the waiter, "in miso vanilla froth. And this is the mache mousse with wasabi beet crackers. And those are your seared whiting on lemon zabaglione. The quail broth is coming."

"And do we have the pork rolls?" said Jackie Farbstein.

"The pork blinis. They're on their way."

"Pork blinis, you know your stuff, my friend. Don't let me confuse you. I'm really looking forward to those. What do you think?"

"It's gorgeous," said Lionel. "I don't know how to eat it."

The blonde from across the room was standing next to Lionel. She was leaning against the corner of the booth, against the banquette that Jackie Farbstein was sitting on, and staring at Jackie. "Which way are the washrooms?" she said to Jackie.

"I am glad," said Jackie, "you decided to say hello. I've been noticing you."

"I know you have." She had a big smile. She wrapped one ankle around the other and put her elbow on the back of the banquette.

"Are you having a fabulous evening?" said Jackie.

"So-so," she said. "You."

"We are. We are having an excellent time. Would you like to join us for a second?"

"I can't. I'm just on my way to the washrooms." She was rubbing her instep against her calf.

"Is that your boyfriend?"

"No no," she said. "He's a friend."

"He's not right for you."

"Oh," she said. "He's very nice. He's." She shook her head, smiling as if at something funny. She was in no hurry to get to the washroom. She said in a low voice, "He's just a rich guy."

"That's what I figured," said Jackie, and they both laughed.

Lionel really wanted to turn around and take a second look at her date. He was only sitting a few feet away. The guy had looked pretty big. Lionel could feel the stare at the back of his neck. But he wasn't going to turn around. He was going to pretend that this was completely polite and normal and inoffensive. He was going to learn how to do this from Jackie Farbstein. So he sat with a stupid smile on his face.

"I like your energy," said Jackie. "You have a terrific energy. What's your sign?"

"What do you think? Guess."

Jackie made a show of pulling back and squinting as he took her in. Maybe he was feeling her energy. "It's a fire sign, I would say, definitely a fire sign."

"No."

Lionel's jaw was clamped shut. He stopped trying to smile and took some more of the rabbit dumplings.

"What about me?" said Jackie. "I should be easy."

"You are easy. Pisces, obviously."

"Nope. Way off."

The rabbit dumplings were really pretty good. While he chewed, Lionel turned his head just a little, as if he were looking around the room for the waiter, to try to glimpse the blonde's date. He was sitting in his seat watching them. His arms were folded.

Lionel felt a little tension in his guts. In Hamilton, Ontario, where he, Lionel, had spent a large part of his childhood, this kind of situation would not be considered good at all, and a guy staring at you like that while a blonde leaned over you so that the ends of her hair brushed the shoulder of your jacket might even make you think of checking out where the fire exits were. But he knew this place was different, and that Jackie could do this anywhere and it would for some reason be all right.

The shredded pork blinis arrived and they smelled of fire and flowers.

"So," said Jackie, "Miss Aries—I don't know about Aries, I don't really see it, but okay—listen—"

"Leo," she said, "I can see it now. You are totally Leo."

"I am. So what is it you do, what kind of business?"

"You know, you haven't even asked me my name yet. Don't you think you should ask me that first?"

"I asked you something else. First."

The girl frowned. She looked over at her date, and for a second it looked as if she was going to leave them. She shook her hair out and took a strand of it between her fingers and said, "I run my own business."

"A P.R. business," said Jackie Farbstein. "Marketing, promotions."

"You're sure about that?"

"Yes, I am. Am I wrong?"

"No. That's about it." She smiled again.

Neither Jackie nor the blonde had looked once at Lionel during this entire exchange, but Jackie looked at him now, and Lionel wondered how Jackie was going to introduce him since he had not yet introduced himself, but Jackie waved his hands over the food and said, "Isn't this beautiful? Shall we eat it?" He turned to the girl and said, "We shouldn't keep you from your table."

She stood up straight and said, with a little surprise, "Yes. I should get back."

"It was a pleasure talking to you," said Jackie, without looking at her. She waited for a second, looking uncertain, and then she turned and disappeared.

"Wow," said Lionel. "That was incredible. That was magnificent."

"Are these the pork things? They any good? Sometimes they can be too sweet, with tamarind."

"I can't get over it," said Lionel. "I have never seen anything like that. It was awesome, I mean literally awesome, I mean I felt awe."

"You just have to feel relaxed about it," said Jackie.

"No, but there was real finesse there. I mean, the thing that really capped it was ending it. I mean you just dismissed her. You told her to run along. It was . . ."

"You have to keep control," said Jackie, "of negotiations."

"Is that why you wouldn't ask her what her name was? Because she wanted you to?"

"Exactly. You keep control."

"You keep all your information secret, until you really have to . . ." Lionel was shaking his head. "It's amazing. It really is."

"It's my business background," said Jackie.

"Is the guy still staring at you?"

"Yup. Now he's looking away. He's just waiting for her to come back. He'll be fine. Do we need more wine?"

At the bar, Edward had finally got down to business. "It's a lovely place," he was saying. "It's about two, two-and-a-half hours north. I'm there most weekends. We generally have a few people up. You should come and see it."

"I would absolutely love to," said Jennifer.

"It's pretty deluxe," said Guntar. "You're going to like it. Big fireplaces, pond, shooting, if you want."

"Hot tub," said Ravi.

"Two, actually," said Edward. "Two hot tubs. One's on the top deck of the main lodge."

"Excellent," said Jennifer. "I love hot tubs. I hope there's no nonsense about bathing suits. I don't see the point of bathing suits in hot tubs."

"Yeah," said Edward. He drank deeply from his beer.

"When can we come?" said Jennifer.

"In two weeks," said Edward, "I'll be back from Boston and I was thinking to go up and chill. You guys both want to come?"

"Two weeks," said Sharon, looking at Jennifer, "I don't think I can. I think I have a thing that weekend."

"That's too bad," said Jennifer, smiling at her.

"You can come on your own, if you like, too," said Edward.

"I'll have to check," said Jennifer. "Give me your card, and I'll get back to you tomorrow, or my assistant will." She put her glass down on the marble and pointed at it. Now she could relax. Maybe they would go over and talk to Olivier and Charles Easton and the new guy Bobby now. From where she sat she could only see the back of his head, but from the way he was sitting he looked pretty straight.

Jackie Farbstein had also finally got down to business. "Well," he said, "I'm glad you asked. This is the thing. The downtown clubs are doing great, no complaints. The people who go to them are maybe not exactly my kind of people or yours, let's face it, and that's okay. I wouldn't go to one of my Richmond Street clubs on a Friday night, to tell you the truth, but I'm happy they're happy, you know what I mean? And the theatre is doing great, too. We're still running Rent uptown and we're about to close the African thing, Ushawa or whatever it is, downtown. That's the big African traditional song and dance thing."

"Umoja. I hear it was terrific."

"Umoja. You know what, it wasn't bad. It wasn't bad at all."

"And I hear you've got this new New York art scene story coming there, what is it?"

"It's called Jacked. I saw it there, and I just knew I had to have it. It's hilarious, it's sharp, it's edgy. I know you don't have much time for musicals, Lionel, but even you might like it."

"It's supposed to be the next hot thing, I know that."

"Well, this is it. I'm glad you recognize that, Lionel. Thank you. I mean, thank you. I am so reassured to talk to you about this. Because you'd think that the theatre press, or whatever passes for theatre press, or any media in this uptight little town, would be able to get their heads out of whatever is tried and true, you know, you'd think they'd be interested in something other than what they saw when they were visiting their cousins in Philadelphia or St. Louis or whatever."

"That's the theatre reviewers," said Lionel. "They want to see the show they saw on the Carnival cruise to Jamaica."

"Exactly. Exactly. I am so glad you understand this."

"So they're not all over this."

"I think it's just that they don't get it. They don't get that this art form has to evolve, it has to break new boundaries. They're stuck in the past. They wouldn't know something good if it—"

"Also," said Lionel, "They probably think you don't need the press. They can be a bit bitchy about success."

"Well, this is what I was wondering. This is one of the reasons, aside from catching up with you, of course, that I wanted to talk to you."

Lionel nodded, relieved to know what it was, finally. "There are some people I can talk to," he said. "I'm doing a talk out at York on the weekend. And a panel discussion on *The Arts Today*, tomorrow. I could bring it up."

"If you wanted to," said Jackie, "that would be extremely helpful."

Lionel went out to the corridor to the washrooms to call Sandra again. This time she was home. He said. "It turns out he wants me to help him get some media excited about his new megamusical."

"And can you do that?"

"I don't know. I can probably spread the word a bit, yeah. I can get him something."

"You hate musicals."

"Deebee—"

"Is he going to pay you for it?"

"Deebee, he has an army of PR people he pays. I'm just going to say I like it to a few people. That counts for a whole lot more."

"And do you want to do that?"

"I don't mind. Deebee, he's a really nice guy. I like hanging out with him. And he's very generous to me. It's the least I can do."

"So you're going to be out for a while longer?"

"Probably, yeah. Why? You want me to be home?"

She said, "Who's there?"

"Who's here? Oh, nobody really. Me and Jackie. A bunch of lawyers, you know Edward whatsisname, the dog food guy. His family is, I mean. I think it's dog food. Maybe it's supermarkets. Something like that. And, let's see, Charles Easton and Olivier and a new guy. I haven't talked to them yet. That's about it."

Sandra's voice was quiet. "Who else."

"You mean women?"

"You know that's what I mean."

"Women. Yes. Jennifer and Sharon are at the bar. They're with the lawyers. That's about it." The blonde came out of the washroom. She and Lionel smiled at each other as she swished past him. Her heels clicked on the hardwood, and Lionel covered the mouthpiece for a second while the sound faded.

"Is that bartender working?"

"Which bartender?"

"The one you say is beautiful."

"I really don't know which one you mean."

Now Sharon was clicking down the corridor. Lionel waved at her. As she passed him she ran her palm across his cheek as you would pet a cat. He stroked her silk shoulder.

Sandra said, "Chrissie, I think her name is."

"Oh, Chrissie. I'm not sure. I think so, yes. She is working." Lionel sighed. "Why? Are you afraid I'm going to run off with the bartender?"

"I just asked if she was working."

"Chrissie is working. Yes. There is also a very pretty hostess tonight. I don't know her name. Do you want to talk to her?"

This is why Lionel did not like calling Sandra from here. This always happened.

"Anyway," he said. "I'll call you when we're done dinner. Do you want to come and have a drink with us after?"

"You know I can't. You know what time I get up."

"Okay. I won't be late."

"Don't be. Call me when you're done dinner."

"Sure."

"I hope Jackie isn't too generous with you."

Lionel pretended not to hear this. He said, "I'll call you."

When he hung up the air was still full of Sharon's perfume. He hung around for a minute to wait for her, because he knew she often carried Ativans or Xanaxes, and he felt the same way now he always did after he talked to Sandra when she was home and he was out. Or whenever he talked to her at any time, these days, really. He would only do a half.

Over by the fireplace, the new guy Bobby was saying to Olivier and Charles Easton, "The names are so evocative. They make me think they all have personalities. Like Xanax, Xanax is some kind of science-fiction superhero. He's swarthy and all dressed in black leather."

"Or a Greek god," said Charles Easton. "Xanax, god of sleep. He's got bright blue eyes, and he's very calming."

"He speaks to you of history," said the new guy, "of battles and, I don't know, great deeds. He is full of wisdom."

"He hangs out with his disciple," said Olivier, "Ativan."

"Ativan. He's slick. He's a hip young guy."

"In a black suit and sunglasses. His handshake is cool to the touch."

"He never takes off those sunglasses, even at night."

"There's something kind of menacing about him, though, some dark underside."

"Ativan, the man."

"Brother of Normacet."

"Normacet. Perky cheerleader type."

"Yes. Pigtails and kilt. Terrific company on long flights, is Normacet, but kind of bland."

"You don't remember too much of her conversation either, afterwards."

"Anyone ever met Imovane? Beautiful, beautiful sad Gothic girl."

Charles and Olivier and the new guy laughed and clinked their glasses.

Jennifer saw this and got up and went over to them. She was extra friendly to Charles Easton and Olivier, and ignored the new guy. She sat on Charles' lap and told him how glamorous he looked. Charles introduced him to the new guy with the short hair, whose name was in fact Robert, not Bobby. It turns out that Charles Easton called him Bobby as a joke, because Robert hated it. His name was Robert Henninger. Jennifer did think that the name Bobby had seemed a little incongruous with his masculine haircut and his old jacket. He also had scuffed shoes and corduroy jeans.

"Have you ever met Imovane?" said Robert Henninger.

"Imovane, the sleeping pill?" said Jennifer. "Oh yes. I have."

"What do you think she looks like?"

"Sorry?"

"We all think she'd be rather dramatic," said Robert Henninger. "And pale."

"She dresses," said Charles Easton, "like the hero of an Edgar Allen Poe story. Velvet cape over her frail shoulders."

"Yes" said Robert Henninger, "and under that a thin nightgown. Her skin is translucent."

"You can see the blue veins on her bony chest."

"She's dangerous," said Jennifer. "She's kind of hysterical. Always weeping, always a drama. You kind of want to get close to her, but you know it's trouble."

Robert Henninger nodded. "Imovane is so dramatic she carries a sort of a prescience of death with her. You feel that if you close your eyes, your sleep will be too deep and carry no dreams."

"Jesus," said Jennifer. "Are you in the TV business?"

"TV? No. Not at all."

"Music, then. You're a musician."

"Music?" said Robert Henninger. "What makes you say that?"

"I have no idea," said Jennifer. "I know some people in the music business. But I don't know you."

"Is it the way I'm dressed?"

"I really don't know."

"I am underdressed in here, aren't I?"

Jennifer smiled. Robert smiled back.

"I'm a student. I don't have a lot of money for clothes."

"What do you study?"

"Bob is a superbrain," said Olivier. "He's the country's biggest expert on the philosophy of poetry."

This for some reason made everybody laugh except Robert. "I guess," said Robert, "that is a bit like saying a very famous croquet player."

Then Sharon had to be introduced, and then more drinks were ordered, and Robert asked her if Fentanyl was here and she didn't get it and so Robert went on a little riff. "Beautiful, mad Fentanyl. With her yellow plaits. Pigtails. Very beautiful. Astoundingly, almost perfectly beautiful. But the odd thing is." He leaned towards Jennifer and looked her in the eyes. "She can come close to you, too close, and not give off any smell or warmth."

"She's dangerous, too," said Olivier. "She might start breaking things at any minute."

"Ah," said Sharon. "I get it."

"She hangs out," said Robert, "with pretty Paxil and trendy Celexa."

"Aha," said Jennifer. "The mod bunch."

"Exactly. They have perfect, pristine condos."

"And no one has any sex in them."

Jennifer laughed. Robert was still looking at her. She felt a little sad for herself. It would be nice if there were a point to having things with guys like Robert. She used to do it all the time. She decided she would let Robert entertain her for a while but she would not let it get too far. She leaned towards him and said, "Tell us about the philosophy of poetry."

When Lionel got back to his table, Jackie Farbstein was standing up and the blonde and the big guy were standing too, and for a second Lionel thought things had turned bad, but as he approached he saw Jackie touch the guy on the arm and the guy nodded, as if he were listening to some useful advice. Lionel stood with them, waiting for the sweet grit under his tongue to dissolve. It was always a bit fizzy, like some kind of sherbet. In five minutes he would feel it in his veins like sleep.

Jackie was saying to the big guy, "This girl, this girl I can tell has a fabulous energy. You guys have a wonderful time tonight. I took care of that last bottle of wine you had."

Lionel waited, ignored, for several minutes while Jackie and the big guy assured each other how terrific and cool each other

was, and then Jackie wished the couple a fantastic night and went
off to congratulate the chef. Lionel said he'd wait in the bar, so he
went and sat down with Jennifer and Sharon and Charles Easton
and Olivier and Robert Henninger. Robert Henninger said to him,
"Lionel Baratelli? Yes. Wow. I went to a seminar of yours once. At
York. You were speaking, anyway."

"Really." Lionel stared at him and did not recognize him. "You
were a student?"

"Not in that class, no. It was my colleague's class. David Winthrup's class. A post-colonial class. I think they were doing your
first novel. I was just sitting in."

"Really." Lionel slumped in his chair a little. There were no
traces of the pill left in his mouth and he still wasn't feeling it.

"I really enjoyed it. Your visit and the novel both."

"Really?" Lionel felt tired. "I haven't heard anyone say anything like that for. Well, for some years."

"Really? I thought you were quite popular. With the students.
It was a big hit."

Lionel looked at Robert Henninger again. He was perhaps a
little bit familiar; one of those earnest grad students who canoes
on weekends and travels in Japan. "You do post-colonial?"

"No, theory. Contemporary poetry, theory."

"Got it. You came to Winthrup's seminar just because you like
my book?"

"Sure. Yes."

"Extraordinary." Lionel was aware that Jennifer was listening
closely to them and looking quite a lot at Robert Henninger and
smiling a little more than was usual for her. He felt a little sorry for
Robert Henninger for a second, if that man was going to pursue
Jennifer, but only for a second, for any reminder of people who
were actually completing a PhD tended to leave him a little unset-
tled; he had to admit this.

"What are you working on now?" said Robert Henninger.

Lionel smiled. "Would you like another drink?"

"Robert," said Jennifer, "Do you work out?"

Lionel went to the bar. He stood there for a while shoulder to shoulder to Edward and Guntar, who were getting a little rowdy.

"Booze," said Edward, slamming an empty beer bottle on the marble. "Boozey. Booze-o. Booze-oh!"

Ravi pushed between them. "Fucking wall-to-wall pussy in here tonight. Wall-to-wall cunt. All right," he called across the bar, "who's going to have to deal with me now?"

Lionel stayed with them for a second and listened as Ravi explained, within earshot of Chrissie the bartender, what kind of tits were best on women and what kind were best on strippers, and how much you could touch them or even suck on them if you were only cool about it.

Lionel noticed that Jennifer and Robert Henninger had separated themselves from the group at the fireplace, and were sitting on two corners of an ottoman. They were not smiling. Normally, Lionel would have left them alone in this situation, but perhaps the pill was working in him, because he sat down on a chair next to them. Perhaps it was simple curiosity, or perhaps he saw something of himself in Robert Henninger and wanted to see him fail.

The conversation he overheard was already quite heated.

Robert Henninger was saying, "So it's kind of a very simple exchange. You get a kind of security with a very dumb guy—"

"Oh, they're not so dumb," said Jennifer. "Not so dumb at all. You sensitive boys always think you're smarter because you don't have any money. I often wonder who is smarter, the sensitive clever boys who read all day long and are really proud that they can't get a job, or the dumb boys who spend fourteen hours a day in an office studying numbers."

"I realize," said Robert Henninger, "I realize that it's not so easy to dominate the world of—"

"What makes you think you're so superior? Because you don't have as much money?"

"I don't feel superior," said Robert Henninger. "I don't feel superior to anyone. I do think my life is a little more interesting, though, than it would be if I were really devoted to making a lot of money. My point is that you're superior. To them. You are. I can tell you are. I can see the way you deal with those guys. I was watching you."

"That's kind of flattering and kind of creepy," said Jennifer.

Lionel was openly listening to them now, and they were both aware of him and they both ignored him. Perhaps they thought he would be some kind of impartial judge, able to explain themselves to themselves. Jennifer even turned and smiled at him.

Lionel was also aware that the young guy with the notebook, who was in an armchair now not too far from them, was staring at them all pretty intently too. For a second it was like a scene in a play.

"It's sweet that you care so much about my future," Jennifer said to Robert Henninger. "But I wonder about your motivations."

"You are right," said Robert Henninger. "I want to ask you out. I did ask you out. That's why we got into this strange discussion."

"I would love to go out with you," said Jennifer gently. She even put a hand on Henninger's knee. "I'm sure we would have a lot of fun. I'm just saving us both a lot of time and effort. And maybe even some sadness."

"You see," said Henninger. "You see how you talk. You're so not like those guys." His face was red now, and he drained his beer. "I bet you'd rather talk about poetry, to be honest."

"I would, yes," she said. "I would. It just . . . if we all had all the time in the world, we'd do whatever we wanted."

"Well maybe if you gave those ridiculous no-money sensitive clever boys a chance, instead of thinking all the time about—"

"Why the fuck." She paused here, her back straight, as if to let Robert Henninger know that this was not a word she used with strangers and she wanted him to notice it. She was staring at him. He was silent. She repeated herself. "Why the *fuck*." She pulled a silver case from her purse and took a cigarette from it. "Would I bother with sensitive boys?" She unwrapped her shiny legs from their skirt-splitting pose and she stood, with the unlit cigarette in her hand. "Think about it. Why would I spend six months teaching a clever boy how to have sex and what wine is and buying him clothes. And letting him teach me about movies and mathematics. And having fun romantic dates in horrendous pubs with the sticky floors, because I have to let him pay for something from time to time and it breaks my heart to see how happy it makes him to play pool in a pub with his friends in their university sweatshirts. And falling in love and pretending I don't care that the bathrooms in pubs stink like piss. And then accidentally introducing him to some girl straight out of school, probably my assistant or something, or even some girl who's never been to school, a waitress, or who's maybe a stripper or something. And see him seduce her with all the skill I have taught him." Jennifer buttoned her little jacket and put the cigarette case in her pocket. She was still holding the cigarette. She was on her way outside to smoke it. "Sensitive boys are so romantic they think they can't be pricks. They think they're not pricks if they're really sensitive, or at least it makes it not so bad or something. Because they're exploring themselves and they're really articulate about it. Anyway. I'm going for a smoke." She picked up the scarf on the back of the stool and she wrapped it around her bare neck and bony chest. "I don't have time, any more. For sensitive boys."

Once she had gone, Lionel and Robert Henninger were silent for a moment. Sharon saw her go and quietly got up to follow her. Charles Easton and Olivier seemed to have missed the whole thing. They were talking about the Oscars.

At length, Henninger said, "Holy fuck."

"Listen," said Lionel.

"What the fuck was that."

"Okay. Listen. It's not you she's mad at. You kind of pressed a button there."

"Holy shit. No kidding."

"I'll be right back." Lionel got up and got Chrissie to pour them two Scotches. He came back and pushed one at Henninger, who accepted it silently.

"Was that about you?" said Henninger.

"No, not really. I don't think so."

"But you did . . . you were once. You had a thing with her."

"A while ago, yes," said Lionel. "No big deal. I wasn't for her."

"Christ." Henninger exhaled with his eyes closed. "I guess everybody in here has slept with everybody else. Is that it?"

"Pretty much, yes. Listen. You just reminded her of something she doesn't like to think about, that's all. And you were wasting your time with her, after all."

"Why? I still really truly don't understand."

"She's thirty-five. That's all that's about. So she's pretty serious right now. About finding some kind of, you know. Something permanent. And she's right. You're too dangerous for her. Attractive is not what she needs right now."

"Well," said Robert Henninger. "I guess that's kind of flattering."

They drank a little Scotch.

Then Henninger said, as if just realizing something, "You mean thirty-five is supposed to be old?"

"She thinks it is. And to be honest, so do a lot of the guys . . . the kind of guy she's interested in."

"But she's gorgeous. She's absolutely stunning."

"Yes, she is."

"I mean, seriously, I saw her and I was knocked out."

"Yes. I know. It's a complicated thing. Those guys, you have to realize those guys can have anyone they want. Models, waitresses, whatever. They're not interested in settling down."

"And Jennifer is."

"There you go," said Lionel. "They told me you were intelligent."

"Dude," said Jackie Farbstein, standing over them. "You ready to go?" He said into his phone, "How long are you going to be there? Are we going to hook up or what?"

"This is Jackie," said Lionel. Robert Henninger stood up and Jackie shook his hand while he talked.

Lionel gestured to his full drink, and Jackie put his hand over the phone and said, "We're going to Julia's thing. She's got a suite at the Gladstone."

Lionel said, "I told Sandra I'd come home."

Jackie raised his eyebrows. "Dude. Julia. You've met Julia. You remember Julia's friends? In a suite. It's the tower suite, I think."

"I haven't seen her all day."

"Dude, Sandra is a very strong woman. I think she'll survive if you, let's say, exercise some initiative tonight." Into the phone, he said, "You don't need to shower. How long is it going to take you to shower? Maybe I can help you." Jackie put his hand over the receiver again and said, "I got her number."

"Whose number."

"The blonde. The one we were talking to."

"What, right now? In front of her date?"

"How?"

"I just asked her. He didn't say a word."

"Kind of a deer in the headlights thing."

"I guess. Hello? So? You want me to come over and dry you off?"

Lionel's trousers vibrated. His phone was in his pocket. He let it buzz. He was on his way home anyway.

Robert Henninger sat again. "This is a bizarre place."

"Yes."

"I'm kind of surprised to meet you here."

"What about you? How did you end up here?"

"I was at school with Easton. He invited me. He told me . . . it's embarrassing. He told me it was a place to meet people."

"Women."

"Yes, women."

They both laughed.

"But also he said it would be good for my career. I might run into people like you here."

Lionel nodded. "Yeah. I'm not so good for your career, really. Listen, you really don't need this place. I don't think it will be good for you. Women like Jennifer . . ."

Henninger laughed. "You were interested in her."

"And look where it's got me."

"No, but really. It's easy for you to say. You have a girlfriend."

"Yes."

Robert Henninger's head was swaying a little. "Well, I want one too. I'm looking for a girlfriend." Apparently he wasn't used to drinking much.

"Girlfriend." Lionel sighed. "Girlfriends are nice."

"See. You have a girlfriend."

"Yes. Wonderful woman. I live with her. It's nice." Lionel took a gulp of Scotch. "But." His phone was still vibrating against his leg. It was never going to stop, like the Tell-Tale Heart. "But it's hard." The phone stopped vibrating. Lionel breathed out.

"Why hard."

"In places like this. To have a girlfriend."

Henninger shrugged.

Lionel said, "Even nice things aren't simple."

"So why come here? What do these people have to talk about? That would interest you?"

Lionel looked around for Sharon and Jennifer. They were still smoking. He could have used another half a pill. He looked back at Henninger, and said gently, as if talking to a child, "There's more to life than talk. I eat very well. I go to lovely houses. I get free trips from time to time. And there are women who look like Jennifer. I've known quite a few of them. But, there you go. You're better off out of it. As you can see. You're not missing anything." Lionel had finished his Scotch. He stared into it to avoid the fact that Robert Henninger was looking at him very hard.

"So what are you working on now?"

Lionel sat way back in his chair. "I'm not really writing any more. Except for magazine articles. Teaching a bit. I do little bits on radio. You know."

"That's sad. You're very talented."

"Thank you."

"No, seriously. I really enjoyed your stuff."

Lionel smiled. He looked around for Jackie.

"No, seriously. Why quit?"

Jackie was at the bar, signing a credit card. He was finally off the phone. Lionel stood up. "It was too difficult. I couldn't stand the reviews. I couldn't stand coming up with ideas. Never knowing if they were any good. I don't have the, I don't know. I don't know what I don't have."

"So what, you're like their tame smart guy now?"

Jackie was back. "Dude. Let's go. Your friends are taken care of too."

"Wow," said Robert Henninger. "That's totally— "

"Don't mention it," said Jackie. "It's a pleasure to meet you. We'd better get going."

In the lobby, Lionel and Jackie gave their tickets to the coat check girl. "I can't come along," said Lionel.

"Lionel," said Jackie, "you're so sweet. You think you'd make a very good husband, but I don't think you're cut out for it. I don't think it's really you, taking orders to get home at a certain time."

Lionel put on his coat. "We didn't say goodnight to the girls."

"They're fine. Listen, I think you should just stop thinking about this. The valet guys are pulling the car up out front. Just get in it and you won't be sorry."

"I'm going home."

"Yes, you are. As soon as you're ready. After we drop in on the girls."

They were waiting for the elevator when Robert Henninger came out and stood with them. "I'm leaving too," he said.

"Good idea," said Lionel. "While you still can."

And then the other guy came out and stood with them, the young guy with the black clothes and the slick hair, who had been writing all night. He carried his black leather notebook with him. He smiled at the other men and they all got into the elevator. It was silent all the way down.

There was a streetcar stop right outside. There was a Filipina lady waiting at the stop. Jackie Farbstein's little black Carrera was waiting for them at the curb. The teenager in the green club jacket was holding the door open for Jackie. Jackie gave him twenty bucks as he slipped into the driver's seat. The teenager went around and opened the passenger door for Lionel.

"I really have to go home," said Lionel.

"Get in," said Jackie.

Lionel's leg started vibrating again. "Shit," he said aloud.

"I'll see you," called Robert Henninger. He was standing at the streetcar stop.

The young guy with the notebook was also standing there. He and Robert Henninger were buttoning their coats up. There was quite a wind coming down the street.

Lionel's trousers buzzed furiously. "Good night, Robert," he said. "It was good to see you."

"You too," said Henninger. "It was an interesting night."

Lionel winced in the wind. He held his coat together. He reached into his pocket and clasped his cellphone, as if holding it tight would stop the vibrations. He walked around the snub nose of Jackie Farbstein's car and got in the passenger side.

The car slid away and Lionel's phone went silent. He looked behind him to see, through the rear window, Robert Henninger and the young guy with the notebook waiting there with the cleaning lady for the streetcar in the dark.

That young man's name was not actually James or William, it was Gavin. And he was in fact, as Sharon had said, related to the Northwoods, which was how he got a membership in that place, but his surname wasn't Northwood, actually, it was Snider.

He hadn't, in the end, written very much tonight. The story he kept meaning to begin had been eluding him. In fact, the last thing he had written in his notebook was, *Surrounded by the successful. Their ease saps mine, drains off my confidence like an infection.* Then he had stopped writing.

Now he was standing at a streetcar stop with Robert Henninger, who of course wouldn't recognize him. He had recognized Henninger and Baratelli both, because he had had Henninger as a T.A. up at York, and he had taken that Winthrup course that Baratelli had come and spoken at. Of course neither of them had recognized him, even though he had asked quite a few questions of each. He wished that he had the confidence to just go up to someone like Lionel Baratelli and tell him he admired him, that he thought his first novel had been brilliant.

In fact, Gavin Snider (that was, remember, this guy's name) had just been about to get up and walk over to Sharon and Jennifer, and reintroduce himself, because he had met Sharon through the Northwoods, but then he had seen the intense conversation with Lionel Baratelli and Robert Henninger and knew he could never compete with that. He had lost his nerve.

Earlier than that, he had also tried talking to Chrissie the bartender, who had been sweet with him, but then he had seen the way that mammoth goof of a barback, the one with the stupid shaggy rock boy haircut, put his hand on her waist, and he knew she was with him or some other guy like him and he didn't have a chance.

What he needed was some kind of confidence. He had confidence in his writing, and that was it. That's where he'd show them. He'd show them confidence. He'd come back tomorrow night, and the night after that, and write down everything he saw.

It was freezing cold. He and Robert Henninger stood there in silence waiting for the streetcar.

RACCOONS

MOTHER'S DAY hung over the house like an appointment for surgery. It was not marked in the calendar of bright Rothkos that hung next to the fridge, but Ivor had seen the smaller daybook that sat on her desk, the square of May 13 marked almost imperceptibly with a tiny *x* in the corner. The day he saw it he felt sick, as if the house was bathed in a childhood smell like granny's lamb or his dad's sports liniment, a warning of punishment.

He would be away on May 13, in Vancouver at a conference on education policy, most of which he would skip to walk on warm streets—dappled with European light and swelling with sunny bosom and calf—and have three beers before dinner, if he ate dinner at all, and watch BBC World in his toddler-free room, and she knew this, his wife did. The trip had already had, at its centre, a dark pit of guilt and now was overlaid by an almost certain failure and subsequent reproach.

He could, he thought, as he stepped into the earth scent of the garage, arrange a brunch on the Saturday before he left, impossible though because he had left all his marking for that day, and had committees all day the Friday. There was the option of a gift and a bunch of flowers—inadequate because too easy; the obligation was to spend time, lots of it, not just money, *commit oneself,* would a little *commitment* be impossible for a man like himself to imagine?

There was a man-sized space inside the garage in which to stand and blink in the gloom and then make out the tower of snow tires and early childhood toys—the yawning Diaper Genie, the training toilet, the never-used rocking horse—and think there, in private, about how the perception of sexual relations had now been forever altered by mommy blogs, and particularly by Kara's own blog, 40YearOldMom, how one could not even think of Mother's Day now without a tone of indignation, of amused slight, imprinting itself on one's language; one could not even approach it without a filter of derision between oneself and the imagining of one's pathetic inadequate actions.

There was a deeper smell to the earth in there, and it was not good, a fecal smell, and this was why he had come in here, to face his suspicion.

At night, Ivor dreamed of his house falling apart. He would be looking up at the newly plastered ceiling and see a dark spot, then reach up to touch it and his hand would sink into damp plaster, and then he would notice how far the stain had spread, the rivulets of brown water running down the walls, the exposed beams, the pewter sky visible. Or it would be the foundation, holes in the floor, a whole wall missing. And he would turn and there would be his father, sitting in the kitchen, unable to help him because of course he had been dead for seven years.

And then he would wake up and hear the scrabbling, as if someone was playing with blocks on a wood floor, just underfoot or in the wall, and he would get up dizzy and realize he was not in his bed but in the daybed downstairs where he was usually exiled at about three in the morning when the Bean slapfooted down the corridor into the Big Bed, warm and whiny, and literally pushed him out. Then the noises would stop. And he would stand at the sliding door to the garden and see shapes in the dark, the striped tails, and be too cowed to open the door and shoo them.

Even when you did, even if you ran at them with your arms out-stretched, screaming your best Monster—making the Bean laugh with the fantastic abandon only available to three-year-olds—they would sit for a second, stare at you, bemused, and then, as if rolling their eyes, slowly turn and lumber away, just before you picked up the brick to chuck at them. (Ivor had actually hit one with a brick once, when the Bean wasn't around, from a distance of about three yards, but only half-heartedly, horrified at himself. The animal had flinched a little, then turned and snarled. The next morning there were piles of dung on both front and back doorsteps.)

And the day before, in broad daylight, an enormous one had lumbered across the upstairs deck right past him, so fat it could hardly haul itself up onto the railing and then the abutting garage roof, utterly unafraid of Ivor's barking and hissing. As he watched it waddle away, then force itself behind the garage (possibly into it?) Ivor realized the swollen girth was unnatural. It was gravid.

So there he was, cellphone and fireplace poker in hand, in the clutter and dark and the spiky smell of foreign feces, looking for slimy babies to kill. They were definitely in there. He stood still.

There was no rustling. There was nothing.

His cellphone was also silent. If it rang in there it might echo and Kara, upstairs with her window open, might hear it. It had already rung twice that morning and she had asked and he had said it was telemarketers, but a third time would not be believable. Now was the time to fiddle with it to figure out the silent vibrate mode thing. He held it up, a little grey flashlight. He checked Kara's updates—she was blogging, up in her room. She had just posted on Facebook, "Weird mood." Five of her friends had asked her what was wrong and she hadn't answered. Then she tweeted, *Remember when you could do whatever you wanted on Saturdays? #endless-work.* And: *Dr. Virpi Lummaa at Univ of Sheffield: research proves sons reduce a mother's life span by an average of 34 weeks. Says nothing about husbands. #sciencefail*

He had to find the vibrate mode, but it was too dark to see the keys, and he hadn't time to find the thing's settings. He just wrapped his fist around it to muffle its inevitable detonation.

There was also a box in there, somewhere behind the Diaper Genie, possibly protected by a sleeping raccoon, that he needed to get to, today, and he needed to find it, identify it among the other boxes, open it and get its contents out and through the house, not just past the raccoon but past Kara, and then into some unrecoverable inferno. He did not know how he was going to do this.

He kicked at some boxes, banged at the metal shelving to scare the animal out.

He listened for breathing.

He began to push at objects, moving them behind him as he worked his way towards the stack of boxes that had been untouched since their move. Behind a CD tower there was another space to stand. The fecal smell was stronger there. There was a dark space between the boxes and the wall that was undoubtedly both a bed and a latrine for unimaginable wriggling vermin. He didn't know which task was more urgent: the uncovering of the monster's lair or the toxic box.

He had not brought a flashlight. He used the phone's screen to look between the stacks.

There was possibly a hole in one wall, covered by boxes, through which they came and went, and with luck they would be out now—where? taking classes? shopping?—although they were supposed to sleep during the day.

He began to pull down boxes. There were CDs, never to be used again, course notes, never to be used again, Christmas ornaments.

Kara's voice from the house. "Ivor? Ivor?"

She knew, she could tell, the second he wanted to be away from her, that he did. She had a sense.

He began ripping open the boxes more quickly. A heavy one, full of kitchen tiles, disintegrated. The tiles clattered.

A backpack containing moldy camping gear. A box of cassette tapes. Closer.

"*Ivor.*"

"Garage," he shouted. "Just checking."

"What?"

Bag of car wax buffers, plus congealed wax. Plywood, assorted shapes.

He put his phone down on a board and the second he did it rang like a siren.

He grabbed it, stifled it, tried to suffocate it.

From the house: "Who is calling you?"

He picked it up; he had to or it would never stop.

"You fucker," said the voice. "You fucking fucker."

"Jasmine," he said as evenly and quietly as he could. "Jasmine, I don't know what you want."

"I am going to firebomb your fucking house is what I want. I know people. You know that? I fucking know people you do not want—"

"Jasmine, please, please, I honestly don't know what it is I did. I really truly don't. And I told you, you can't call here, I live here with my wife and my—"

"Oh I can't? I can't? I can't call there?" There was a pause and a sucking sound, for she would have a joint going now, of course at eleven in the morning. "You think I won't find your other number? Your land line? You watch me fucking call it, you watch me call your fucking wife."

"Okay. Okay. Listen. What do you need from me?"

From the house: "Ivor?," then "Daddy!"

"Oh you have no idea. You have no fucking clue. You are a liar. You are a fucking liar."

"Is it about the tapes? If it's about the tapes I am looking for them right now, right this second."

"Oh now you're smart, now you remember. Because I am going to burn down your fucking house, now you remember."

"You know these tapes are useless, right, to anyone without the exact same camera which is now completely obsolete? To play them you need a VHS tape player and then you need a special adapter to put the little tape in and then put it in the machine, and nobody has that machine or that adapter, anywhere, ever. So this is a complete waste of everyone's time."

"How do I know you haven't copied them?"

"It's impossible to copy them. I would have to take them to a place, one of those places where you pay—and, Christ, this is ridiculous, I haven't looked at these tapes for two years, why would I do that?"

"Why do you have them then?"

Ivor covered the phone and yelled, "One minute!" He kicked at a metal trunk to make it sound as if he was working in there. "Listen," he said to Jasmine, "I am finding them, now. And when I find them I am going to destroy them. I have no need for them at all, I promise you."

"Oh no. Oh no you won't destroy them."

"I won't?"

"I don't trust you for one second, you skunk."

"Jesus." Ivor sat on a canister that looked like a case of grenades but that probably held Duplo Lego. "Jesus, Jas. What do you want?"

"You are going to bring them to me. Today." There was a noise of daytime TV, a giggly commercial.

"Today is not possible. It's Saturday. I am with my family."

"Today, like now. You are not going to have any time to copy them and put them on the internet or use them in any disgusting way."

"Jasmine, Jesus, I have absolutely no interest in doing that."

"You bring them to me in one hour or there are going to be fucking consequences."

The TV and her voice were gone. He put the phone in his pocket.

He opened boxes quickly then, boxes of school binders and medical records, boxes of tax. He moved an umbrella stand and a plastic wading pool. There were no more boxes. It had possibly been thrown out in the move. That would be bad.

It occurred to him that if he could not find the box, it might be time to think about calling the police. But this would entail a frank discussion with Kara that would be unimaginable at any time, let alone in the full flooding anticipation of Mother's Day.

He moved a bag of charcoal briquettes. They had not had a charcoal barbecue for three years. He put the bag of charcoal beside the bags of topsoil and grass seed. It was at least more coherent there, a bag among bags.

He kicked the topsoil bag and it broke and its black powder ejaculated. He said "cockpoop shit." When he bent to sweep the earth with his bare hand he saw it, the blue hat box with the white strap, under the weight bench. He had to lay himself flat on the dusty floor to reach under.

He sat on the weight bench to open it. There was the clunky black camera, the battery the size of a juice box. It would probably be dead. And under it the blocky little Hi-8 cassettes, all labelled innocuous things like "Davenports' cottage" or "Hockey Brampton." Under each title he had marked in pencil his tiny x's. Sometimes an almost invisible J.

The camera opened like a book, the viewing screen folding outwards. He picked a tape—"City parade 2002"—that had two pencil x's. It slid into its cage, and amazingly the red power light came on. He pressed play.

There was the green room, her basement room, and there she was, pale and smiling and delicious, bare-legged, on her stained bed, running her hands through her hair, smoking a joint. He knew every second of this tape, knew exactly when the voice off-camera, his voice, embarrassingly squeaky, would say, "Take your top off," and her smile then, the sunniest, most open smile, a smile of love and abandon, as she crossed her arms to pull the fabric upwards. He had watched this tape at first to see her body emerge, over and again, in its pallor and its vulnerability, to see the coin-sized yellow

132 CONFIDENCE

bruise on her ribcage, the quiver of her belly, and the sheer joy she had at exposing herself for him.

And then after a while he had only watched the beginning, to see that smile, a smile indicating a pleasure he had never caused anyone else to experience.

"Daddy," said a voice close to him, "what you doing?"

"I'm cleaning, sweetie. I'm cleaning up. Tell your mother I'm cleaning up." He had snapped the screen shut and dropped the camera back into the box in one motion.

"What's that?"

"Nothing. Old toys I'm throwing out."

"I want them. Let me see."

"No, you don't. They're not yours."

"All the toys are mine."

The Bean had a point here.

"I'm going to clean this up and then I'm going to go in the car to give them away to the Salvation Army."

"To the poor people?"

"Yes. So go inside and—"

"No. I want my toys."

"They're baby things. You're not a baby, are you? Now go inside and tell mummy that's what I'm doing."

"It's a camewa," said the Bean, pointing at the hatbox. "Let me see it."

"No." Ivor pushed it away with his foot. "Now go tell mummy—"

"It's a camewa!" the boy squealed. "Let me make a movie!"

"No, it doesn't work. Listen, I'm looking for raccoons. Do you think there are raccoons in here?"

The boy stepped back, into the sunlight. "No. No."

"They are a little scary. I think I'd better look for them on my own."

"I want to see them." But he was backing away.

"No, you don't. Go inside and tell mummy I haven't found them yet."

"When you find them, will you kill them?"

"No, no, of course not."

"Do we eat them?"

"No."

"And if you kill them they will be in the sky."

"No, they won't. I won't kill them."

"Will they come inside?"

"No, they won't."

"What will they do?"

"They will. Ah. I'm not sure yet."

"Daddy, what will you do? What will you do?"

"Ivor." And there was the tall shadow of Kara. "I've been calling you for ages."

He stepped into the light to block her way. "I haven't found them yet," he said, "but I know they're in here."

"He's not going to kill them," said the Bean.

"So I'm off now," said Kara.

"What I'm going to have to do," said Ivor, "is clean this thing out a bit. There are a bunch of things I'm going to take to the Salvation Army. All these old baby things. I can go right now."

"Daddy," said the Bean, "what is called crack cocaine?"

Ivor and Kara were quite still for a moment. Then he cleared his throat. "What is what?"

"Crack cocaine."

He kneeled and looked in the boy's eyes. "Where did you hear that word?"

"The report man said the mayor was smoking crack cocaine."

"Yes that is right. He said that."

"What is crack cocaine?"

The sun was in Ivor's eyes and his knees burned. Kara was moving into the shed. "Where are they?" she said.

"Crack cocaine is poison," said Ivor. "Right mummy? It's a poison and it's very bad for you."

"And you smoke it?"

"No, you don't. If you touch it, you have to go to hospital. And the police will come and take you to jail. That's why everybody is very very mad at the mayor."

"Why did he smoke it?"

"Well, we don't know if—"

"The report man said the mayor smoked crack cocaine. And but, but, but, but, but, but, but."

"Okay," said Ivor.

"But the mayor said he didn't smoked it. Doesn't smoked it. And, and, and, and, and, and, and, and, and."

"Yes."

"And I think he's lying."

"Yes," said Kara, "he is lying. Sometimes grown up men lie."

"Okay buddy," said Ivor. He stood up, cracking. "I'm going to get ready to go now. Kara—"

"Ivor," she said, standing in the dankness and shading her eyes, "Sweetie, you know when you tidied up all the sunglasses that were on the chest, that now I can't find mine, the prescription ones?"

He could smell calendula moisturizer on her, as if she had washed her hair in it. "I just moved them, my love, I put them all inside the bicycle helmet that's in the trunk."

"But you didn't, they're not there."

"Daddy," said the Bean, "Let's pretend let's pretend we're Mounties." He had grabbed a club, a piece of the old fencing that Ivor had yet to remove, and was waving it.

"Okay sweetie."

"And we're looking for dragons. On the racetrack. And they're Hondas."

Ivor said, "I assure you I didn't move any sunglasses away from there, I promise you that. I would have no reason to move your sunglasses."

" But you did, you just said, you moved them."

Ivor let out a burst of air. "I kept them all together. I promise you I would have no reason to move your sunglasses. What would my reason be for doing that?"

" I don't know, but I know that I left them there and they're not there now."

With her back to him, he nudged the hat box further under the weight bench with his foot. He said, "I see. I see. What is your theory, exactly, as to what I did with them, or have reason to do with them?"

"What?"

"Your theory. What is your theory. That I took them, removed them from where they were sitting and hid them from you? There would have to be some malice involved in that. Quite a lot of malice."

"Daddy, let's pretend we're in Chicago."

"What are you so angry about?" said Kara.

"I'm not angry. I'm not angry. Listen, I'm going to load a bunch of things into the car. I'm going to scoot them down to the Salvation Army."

"Now?"

"Yes, why not? I'll get it done before lunch and then I can take this fellow for the afternoon and you can do your mindfulness."

"Are you crazy?"

"Daddy," said the Bean, "can a Honda fight a bear?" He slammed his stick into the side of the metal shed. This was very loud.

"Are you absolutely crazy?"

"Daddy's not crazy."

"I have told you three times I'm out with Julianne this afternoon."

"That's this afternoon? Beanie, stop that."

"What is distracting you today?"

"Beanie, stop it right now."

"Daddy, are you crazy?"

"I'm doing my mindfulness right now, and then you have him all afternoon."

"Oh, good. Fine."

"Don't bore him by taking him to the stupid Salvation Army. You have to entertain him, you have to be—"

"Daddy! Daddy!"

"Not now, Beanie, mummy's talking."

"Daddy! Mummy said stupid!" The boy was jumping and pointing.

"Yes, she did, and she shouldn't."

"Oh for God's sake," said Kara.

"Everything's fine," said Ivor. "You go now and do your thing. We'll play out here."

"I'm not going to tell Marianna," said the Bean.

"What's that?" said Ivor, bending again.

"I'm not going to tell Marianna mummy said stupid."

"No, you don't have to. Sometimes grownups can say stupid."

"It stinks in here," said Kara.

"I think that's the raccoons."

"Daddy, can you say hate?"

"Who says hate?"

"Mummy."

Ivor exhaled again. "Listen," he said to her, "you're right about not taking him to the Salvation Army. So I'll just go on my own now, really fast, I'll be there and back in an hour, and you can start your—"

"Are you completely smoking crack? We planned all this yesterday. I am on my way out now."

"Daddy, are you smoking crack? Is Daddy smoking crack?"

"Beanie," said Ivor, "if you don't stop banging that thing right this second I am taking away your blue tow truck, the big one."

There was a second of silence before the Bean's face folded up into its mask of misery and he began to wail. Kara put her hands over her ears and walked towards the house.

Ivor called after her: "That's a nice shirt."

She shouted back: "*Nothing!*"

"What?" he said with genuine puzzlement.

She stopped on the path. "Oh," she said. "I thought you were accusing me of something."

After she left he made the Bean a grilled cheese sandwich and sliced red peppers, then melon balls and sliced pears, none of which the boy ate. The peppers he threw with some force onto the carpet. The sandwich he took with him for a run around the ground floor and halfway up the stairs; Ivor found it later stuffed under the sofa. He made a train track out of the pear slices and then cried when he was told not to. He drank two glasses of milk and demanded gummy bears and apple juice, and cried hysterically when denied them.

When Ivor was cleaning up after this, his phone rang again.

Her voice, raspy, as if on the edge of shouting. "When are you getting here?"

"I told you, I can't today. It's impossible."

"You are getting here today. You are getting here right now."

"Or what?"

He heard her breathing. Too fast. The television snarling as if in pain. She disconnected with a bang.

"Christ," said Ivor.

"Daddy, was that the police?"

"The police? Why would it be the police? No, sweetie. It wasn't the police. Listen, we're going to go for a drive in the car now."

In the car the Bean sang the morning song, which went, "The good morning train is coming, choo-choo. We say good morning to Bernard, choo-choo. We say good morning to Jamal, choo-choo. We say good morning to Tsao, choo-choo. We say good morning to Asha, choo-choo. We say good morning to Aqif, choo-choo. We say good morning to Yumiko, choo-choo." This song had to be completed in its entirety according to ritual.

But the moment the news came on the radio and Ivor instinc-tively turned it up, the Bean went silent, for of course it was all about the mayor and crack cocaine. Ivor could feel the stories imprinting on the little brain as if on wet concrete. The idea that the mayor smoked crack cocaine, whatever that was, was like a first series of commands that were going to become part of the boy's operating system; they would be hardwired like the idea that you can't say stupid or that boys can't wear pink or that you say grace before every meal (which must have come from Marianna, at day-care, against all regulations no doubt, but what could you do when you entrusted your child's socialization to peasants?)

"Daddy, is he lying?"

"Well, we don't know, Beanie. We don't have any proof."

"What is called proof."

"Proof is evidence. Evidence is when you know something. They have no video evidence." As he said this he put his hand over the hatbox in the front seat, as if to restrain it from flying out the window. He didn't know why he did this. He was eager to get it out of the car and away from the boy. "Look, a Jeep."

"Thass not a Jeep. Thass a Subaru."

"So it is. Good for you."

"What is called proof."

"I just told you."

"Why."

"Okay."

"Daddy why."

"Okay then."

"Daddy, are the police going to come?"

"Why do you—listen, the police aren't going to come for any-one, all right? Nobody is in any trouble. Not even the mayor."

Her door was in an alley, at the side of a house; it led to a base-ment. So he could nose down the alley and park the car right there, leaving, he hoped, the narrowest of gaps for passing, and leave the

Bean strapped in his seat and just do the exchange at the door. He wouldn't even have to go in. He could possibly even leave it running.

But when he arrived, there was a car in the spot. He parked behind it. But then he wouldn't be able to leave the Bean in the car because he wouldn't be able to see him from the door. He sat there for a minute thinking about this.

He checked his phone. 40yearoldmom had just tweeted, *When husbands move around a couple of boxes in the garage, do they expect the rest of the day off? #mommytime #entitlement*

"Daddy, what are we doing."

"I'm just going to drop these things for poor people, like I said."

"Where are the poor people."

"In this house here. This is the Salvation Army. The door is where you leave things."

"What's the ssavayshinuhmee."

"It's a church, and they give things to poor people."

"Where's the church?"

"There's a lady—there's someone here. I'll be right back, okay?"

Quickly, he grabbed the hat box on the front seat, and slipped out. He looked behind him and saw the Bean's eyes wide and sad.

"Daddy!"

"I'm going to be right back. I'm going to be one minute."

"Daddy. Daddy!"

"Yes."

"My name is Instagram."

"Okay sweetie."

"No, no, no, my name is fire escape."

"Yes it is. Now sit tight here, and I'll be—"

"Daddy, what's a capybara?"

"Okay. I'll be right back."

He slammed the door without looking at those guilt-squeezing big eyes and walked to the door. It was only about ten yards from the car to the front door but still he couldn't keep a close eye on the Bean. He could see the side of the car but not the Bean's face. He rapped hard on the door.

Inside, the television roared murder.

Ivor knocked twice before it opened. She opened it and stepped away. He said, "Here," and held out the box. "I can't stay. My kid's in the car."

She left the door ajar and walked away. The flat smelled of weed smoke and litter box.

"I can't stay," he said. He saw her flop onto her sofa in the dimness, light another joint. The scrawny cat jumped on her lap. She was wearing a flimsy tank top and grey sweatpants, and bare feet. Her eyes were red. But her hair was its usual glossy massive clean spray. He wanted to put his nose in it. "Here." He opened the top of the box and pulled out the camera. "You can have the camera too."

"All right. Let's see them."

The place stank of catshit.

"You have to get up and come over here." He looked over his shoulder at the car. He could see its side but couldn't see or hear the Bean. "I have to watch my kid. In the car."

"I can't get up or Zero will run out the front door," she said, stroking the cat. "She'll run outside. Bring your kid in here."

He almost laughed. "No."

"Oh, what, it's not his class, kind of thing?"

"Jesus. Look. Take them. They're all here."

Slowly, she got up, the joint between her teeth, holding Zero, dumped him in the bathroom and closed the door. Then she took a long suck of her joint, put it down and stretched, her arms above her head. This caused her nipples to be displayed through her stretchy top and her shaved underarms to be revealed. Then she began gathering her hair in her hands and working it into a ponytail. She took her time about this. Finally she moved to him and began to pick through the tapes in the box he held out to her. She did this at arm's length, with her fingertips, as if they were both getting too close to something radioactive.

"They're all here," he said. "I have to go."

"Let me count them."

"Why do you want them so badly?" he said. "They're my memories too."

"If you have them, then you have me," she said. "You can use me, my body, any time you want. And I don't want you to have me."

"But of course I have you. I will always have you."

"That's disgusting."

He thought he perhaps heard the boy shout, so he was silent, craning his head around again. The car was motionless. "What about postcards, I have to destroy those too?" he said. "Or notes? Or photos of the two of us in the Walmart parking lot? Is it disgusting for me to keep those too?"

"And you," she said, "said you don't want me. So you can't have me."

"Okay," he said, "fine. By the way, you can't have them either."

"What?" She was close enough he could smell her hair now, a green appley smell from the stuff she used.

"You're not going to just keep them," he said. "Then you could use them against me."

"What?"

"Yup. If I can't have them then you can't either."

"What do you want me to do?"

There was a car coming down the alleyway, he could hear it. He stepped back and twisted to look: a big SUV pushing its way through, slowing to slide by his parked car with the Bean sitting there. He said, "You're going to destroy them right now, and I'm going to watch you."

"How?"

He put his head into the dim room, looked around. The sink was full of dirty pots and plates of caked cat food, and soapy water.

"Throw them in there, in the sink, then pull the tape out. Get them wet."

"Wow, you are really crazy, you know that?"

He laughed again. "I'll leave that alone," he said. "Just do it. Or I'm taking these back."

"Fuck," she said, viciously, "fuck's sake," and he could feel her rage rising again.

"Just do it. Now."

She grabbed the box roughly and dumped all the contents, including the camera, into the soapy water. The water slopped onto the floor. The tapes floated.

"Destroy them," he said.

She sighed and, swearing, began to rip at the cassettes, pulling out the copper strands. Soon the sink was a tangle of wet filament and cat food. In all of those ribbons were the taste of her, all the high afternoons and the weepy mornings with his mouth full of her. All the rainbow of her undergarments was turning to mud in the sink.

She said nothing.

He said, "All right? Happy? Are we done now?'

"Get out of here."

"Oh, you're welcome. You're very welcome."

"Go."

"Is there anything else you want from me?"

"You leave me the fuck alone."

He laughed for real then. "Okay. Okay. That's funny. I'll leave you alone." He stepped back into the alley, the light.

She came to the door. She leaned against the frame, her hands behind her back, her chest pushed out. She said, "What's your boy's name?"

He said, "Bernard."

"That's a nice name," she said, and her voice quivered. He saw her mouth tense as if she was about to cry and he turned quickly so as not to see it. He ran to the car without looking back.

When he pulled out and past her door it was shut.

"Now," he said to the Bean when they were on the street, "now we're going to go to the other Salvation Army, and drop these things off. And you can tell mummy we just went to the Salvation Army, that's all."

"And there was a lady there?"

"You can tell her there was a lady at the Salvation Army, sure. There are often ladies there. Ladies to take the things you give."

"Who was that lady?"

"Did you see a lady?"

"No."

"Ah. Did you finish the morning song?"

"Daddy, what is ingredients?"

"Ingredients are—"

"What is fascinating?"

"Fascinating is very, very—"

"Ingredients!" shouted the Bean in the back of the car. "Fascinating!" And Ivor drove on to the Salvation Army, where they dumped the Diaper Genie and the portable toilet and the rocking horse, a process that made them both cry.

That evening he was a great husband. He loaded and unloaded the dishwasher, he scrubbed the pots, he carried loads of the Bean's laundry from the basement and got the Bean to help him fold and stack the tiny underpants and socks and the shirts covered in dinosaurs that made him so emotional in a hysterical, non-euphoric way. They did this while singing chain-gang work songs of Ivor's invention, which the Bean found hilarious. And then he volunteered to give the boy a bath and read him stories. He did this very cheerily, telling Kara that he didn't mind because she must be exhausted after her long day with the mindfulness and then Julianne. And didn't the mindfulness make her sleepy?

She was on her tablet most of the evening. Ivor checked his phone periodically to read her posts. There was a long entry on trust in marriage and why access to each other's email accounts was evidence of trust. Then there was a funny story about trying on new bras. There were a couple of tweets: *You may see a messy house, but I see an artistic expression of the chaotic nature of modern society #acceptance #housework.* And: *How many calories does telling people you're on a diet burn? #glutenfreeforever.* And: *If I get really skinny, will my sex drive come back? #cureformotherhood #nolibido*

When it was time to kiss the boy goodnight she said, "What did you guys do all afternoon?"

Ivor said, "Didn't you see? We took all that stuff to the Salvation Army."

"Was that fun for you, Beanie?"

"We had great fun, didn't we Bean? Let's go, up to bed now."

"And to the lady," said the Bean.

"Aren't you pleased?" said Ivor. "The shed is all emptied out now. I feel a great relief, I feel lighter."

"A lady?" said Kara, kneeling.

"There was a lady who took the stuff, at the Salvation Army," said Ivor, tugging on the boy's hand. "Let's do your teeth." He looked down at him with a firm smile on his face, and the Bean looked up at him with cool eyes. He gave a little smile and almost imperceptibly nodded. "Good boy," said Ivor. "Good boy. I love you."

He actually had him halfway up the stairs when the Bean stopped and said, "Daddy, what is called when you look in someone's eyes?"

"Come on, sweetie, no stopping on the stairs."

"What's it called, Daddy?" said the Bean, motionless, "When you look inside someone's eyes."

"Bernard, I'm going to count to three."

"What is it, sweetie?" Kara called from the kitchen.

"It's called luff," said Bernard. "Daddy, let's do luff. Look inside my eyes."

"Okay baby," said Ivor, almost floating with relief. "We'll do luff in bed."

When he came down Kara was watching a model competition show. He thought he would try to watch it for once. He sat and said, "Who's winning?"

She switched off the TV in answer.

"Okay," he said.

"Do you want to chat?"

"About what?"

She turned her face to the black screen and was quiet.

He gave this a minute. Then he said, "What is it?"

"Ivor," she said quietly, "do you ever lie to me?"

"Why do you ask that?"

"You don't answer my question."

"The phone calls today," he said. "It was her. You're right."

"Why didn't you talk to her?"

"I did, actually."

She stiffened beside him. "I see."

"I had to. She kept calling. She wanted help."

"Oh for Christ's sake. When does she not want help."

"I know. And I was very firm today. I was very tough. I told her I couldn't help her any more and she would have to find someone else."

"What was it this time?"

"Oh," he said, leaning his head back and shifting his body towards the television. "Her computer again. It's always broken. Turn it back on. I would watch this one."

"And she knows no other men, no other people to help her with her computer."

"Well, that's what I said. Anyway, it's done. I was firm. And I think this time . . . I am quite confident, anyway, that she won't be calling here again. I told her you didn't like it and that seemed to convince her." He breathed out, waited.

"If she calls here one more time," said Kara, "I'm going to call her back, and tell her to leave us alone."

"Okay," said Ivor. "That's fine. I am quite confident that won't happen."

She sat for a second, and then picked up the remote. When the TV went back on, Ivor settled back with the beginnings of what could have been actual relief. And by the time they had both commented on a girl who looked a little horsey and one who might be a little masculine and one who had what could possibly have been a scar under her eye, it was relief like aspirin to a headache.

And when the show ended and he suggested they not watch the news because they had all been hearing the news all day and they knew it would be just the same accusations and denials about the mayor, she surprisingly said yes and she snapped off the set and stretched and yawned, he knew that they were through the crisis; his boy was sleeping and healthy, if mad, happily mad, upstairs, and they were safe in their home. And it was he, Ivor, strong protector, who had shielded his family from the threat. He almost wanted to tell Kara, so proud was he of himself, but Kara might not be so proud.

She went up and he said he would be right behind her.

Once he heard her brushing her teeth he switched on his tablet, in the darkness of the living room, for actually he couldn't resist checking to see if there were any new developments in the drug-taking mayor story. There weren't, and he found himself hoping that actually the drug tape would never be found, for he felt sorry for the guy, an obese guy with enough stress in his life who had just wanted to do something fun for once, who had just wanted to be with some cool tough guys in a place far away from his suburban house and his family, a place with no decisions and no women, and who could be harmed by this? If all of us had the video of our addictions exposed then there would be no more comfortable houses littered with soap bubble guns and markers, no more children sleeping in beds under steam-engine wallpaper.

He was stretching himself when he heard a tapping, as if someone was at the window. He looked out the window at the narrow alley between the houses and saw nothing. He went to the sliding doors to the backyard and looked there too. There was a thump and more tapping from somewhere close and he stood still to listen.

As he listened the kitchen seemed darker than before. It was a scratching, and some rustling, extremely close, possibly from inside the kitchen cupboards. His heart was beating quite fast now, and he opened the cupboard doors and sprang back, as if something might squirt out at him from in there, but there was nothing.

The slithering was from the wall, from inside the wall. And an insistent crackling, the sound of insulation being removed, clawed or chewed, the sound of his house's guts being devoured.

His phone bleated in his back pocket.

He brought it quickly to his ear, without thinking. "Hello," he said, and regretted it.

"Fuck you," she said.

"Fuck me. Jasmine, why? Why fuck me."

"You know why."

"I do not. Jasmine, I do not. I did everything I could for you today, and now we are—"

"No you did not. You tricked me, again, you snake, you fucking ghoul."

"I honestly have no idea what you are talking about. I did the last thing I can do for you today."

"I found you out. I know what you did."

He did not answer this because he wanted silence so that he could hear where they were, exactly, in the walls. Perhaps they had come down from the attic. Perhaps they were in the heating ducts.

"I looked at the tapes after I let the water out. Of the sink. And I saw the labels. Those weren't the tapes of us. You gave me bullshit tapes."

"Oh, shit. Jasmine. Of course the labels were different. They were fakes. I called them different things. To disguise them. Don't you understand? Everyone does that."

"Why should I believe anything that comes out of your mouth? Everything you say is a lie. It always has been."

"Look more closely at the labels, Jas." He was whispering as loudly as he could. Overhead, more dark footsteps: those were of his wife. "Look at them, you'll see little x's I put in pencil. That's my code. The other things are just to throw people off."

"See?" she said, inhaling simultaneously. He waited for her to expel the weed smoke. "See? Everything's a fake. Everything you touch is a lie."

"Jasmine. I don't know what to tell you. Except that not everybody wants to hurt you. Not everybody is lying to you. Why would they do that? What would be in it for them?"

"I'm looking at one right now," she said. He could hear the music and shouting of a television. "It says Professional Development Day. This one says Market. So where are our tapes?"

"You see, Jas? You see? Those titles are so boring. That's why I wrote them. Listen to me. Those are bullshit titles. Look for the x's."

"It's too late for that."

"Too late?" Overhead, still footsteps, his wife still awake, and now a thumping underfoot. Under the floorboards? He said, "Why is it too late?'

"I burned them. I burned them all. I dried them off, I soaked them in lighter fluid, and I melted them all. Your fucking family tapes."

"Okay, good, I'm glad to hear that. Now there is no trace, no trace whatever of our relationship."

"Oh yes there is. You have them, and I'm coming to get them."

He tried saying her name several times but she had disconnected.

Kara was behind him, ghostly in a white nightie. "Were you on the phone?"

"No. Quiet."

"What?"

"Listen."

They stood facing each other in darkness. She said "What is it?" and he shushed her again. There was the shuffling, and the cracking of something plastic. In the walls.

Together they moved to the sliding glass doors. He double-checked the locking handle. He snapped down the locks on the windows to either side. Then the two of them stood in the windows, looking into the black garden, trying to make out which moving shadows might have been fur, and whether there were any masks in the darkness, looking in at them. He reached his hand toward her and she took it.

SLEEPING
WITH AN ELF

THEIR FAVOURITE RESTAURANT they called the Elf, not because that was its name—its name was something as trying-too-hard as Harvester or Barbershop or Bicycle Shed—actually Bicycle Shed was what they called it too, sometimes, because there were bicycles and tractor parts hanging on the walls, or sometimes they just called it Beards, as when they asked each other, do you want to see beards tonight? Its real name was not well known because of course it was not displayed anywhere; to have a sign on the window in that neighbourhood, at that time, was to admit to an unseemly ambition; you might as well have put up a sign saying Franchise, Inc (actually, they agreed, that would be an extremely clever name). They called it the Elf because there was an elf who worked there. He really did look exactly like an elf in a Christmas drawing: he was just over five-feet tall, it looked like, even in his lace-up boots, and extremely skinny and pointy and tiny in all regards, and wore a tall wool toque, in all weather and even in the heat of the open kitchen as he darted in and out from behind the counter carrying tall beers made from local hops and spring water with labels printed on threshing machines, and house-smoked pork bellies and taro chips and bacon-salted brussels sprouts, his stringy little arms all knotted up and his tiny tattoos writhing; his nose was hooked and even his ears seemed a little too large and upright for his body, holding up the enormous black wool cap like trestles. The elf never spoke to Dominic and Christine, or to anybody; he was an angry elf, and that seemed natural, part of the decor too, like the host with the moustache waxed into curlicues and the meticulously banal folk music on the sound system.

"So where would you meet yours?" said Christine. "Online?"

Dominic did not answer, partly because he did not want to— of course he would go online, like everybody else, but he was not ready to talk about his part in the dangerous game, he was only ready to hear Christine's—and partly because he was trying to swivel his body around a few degrees so he could get at least a glimpse of the tables to his right where he thought he had seen Concetta Accoglienza sitting with a tightly clad young woman possibly her daughter. This operation made him wince, because of his stupid fucking hip and knee and whatever the fuck was fritzing out or rotting or disappearing in his nerves. His cane was gone, taken away with his coat and hooked onto a rack near the entrance. He was going to try to do without the cane if he had to make it past the kitchen to the washroom. Which was good, he could be stronger, he could try to do without it more, and Christine hated seeing him with it.

"Don't look at her," said Christine. "Don't you want to play the game?"

"At who?" he said almost automatically, and then, "Yes, sure, I love the game." Which was true, and it was what they were there for, to play the dangerous game; it was exciting in a place like this, flashing with bodies and strangers, exactly what the dangerous game was all about. "Wait a second, the idea is we're going to talk about who we're going to sleep with, and I can't turn around and look at a girl?"

"It's Concetta Whatever's daughter, it must be, they look identical. You can't stare at girls no matter what I'm talking about because it's rude no matter what. What's her name, Lachupacabra, what? It's a crazy name. What about her, Concetta? She's nice, she likes you, you like the older ladies."

"Can't stare at girls when you're talking, can't do this, can't do that. But I should do this."

"Oh, lighten up. I'm just suggesting."

"I should have sex with Concetta Accoglienza. See, it's not hard to pronounce. Do you want me to?"

Christine shrugged. "I'm just suggesting. I'd be okay with it. What's the matter? You look like you're taking a big shit."

"I'm hurting. Sorry. Not supposed to talk about that." He was hurting, but he was also eager to turn the conversation away from sleeping with Concetta Accoglienza because of course he had already slept with her, more than once, but not for a long time, years ago, in those days when he and Christine were hurting each other so ferociously. And before Concetta had come into the money and started the art foundation and married the developer and gone directly out of Dominic's league. It was still not something that Christine needed to know.

"You want to go home?"

"Of course not. This is trying, like I promised. This is me trying."

"Try to have fun."

"I could have more fun if you'd let me at least look to see who is here. I want to see the costumes." Feeling the sparks up his spine, he pulled his hips around and sat facing the room and the front door.

Everyone was pointy and small in there, including Dominic and Christine. Dominic was feeling particularly small since he had hurt his hip, or had whatever mysterious thing had happened, his nerves mysteriously dying for no reason any of the endless tests could discern. He was still bigger than the elf. "Oh," said Dominic, "oh, look, this guy's too good, a farmer, do you see the farmer? By the window?"

He looked and Christine looked at a guy, a bearded guy who couldn't have been older than twenty-three, sitting with his legs stretched out into the waiter's path, a guy with a heavy wool sweater, and tweed trousers and a tweed cap and knee-length Wellington boots.

"He has to sit that way so everyone can see the boots," said Christine. "Without the boots it's just casual wear. Look at the girl."

The girl with him was not from an Irish bog in a fashion spread about tweed, she was from a city, but from another city, a city in the 1940s. She had the pencil skirt and the glossy black bangs and the blouse with the puffy sleeves, and the line up the back of her stockings and the chunky shoes. Her lips were the sharpest outline of red in the room, except perhaps for Concetta Accoglienza's.

"It's good," said Dominic, "it's a Rosie the Riveter thing."

"It's a pinup thing. She has tattoos. Anchors and that."

"She does burlesque. God help us. When will it die."

"God save us from burlesque," said Christine, "and the lectures of fat girls."

"It's hilarious," said Dominic. "I wouldn't be surprised if the next guy that came in was a pirate. Then Louis the Fourteenth. What are you going to be?"

"Sad clown."

"Sexy cop. Robot. Bumblebee."

Through the big garage-door front window they could see women passing who were dressed as prostitutes, because they were. It was Friday night. The prostitutes, sadly, would all be gone soon, if there were more places like the Elf, which would be very good for Dominic's property value but much less good for his sense of romance, of being alive. Strange how prostitute was never a costume you'd ever see in here, in the Elf.

Across the street was the white fluorescence of Djibouti Cafe and Restaurant (Business Club), thank god still there. It was never romantic in there or just outside it.

"Hey, there's Frederick, at the bar." Dominic waved at the hunched figure in his black hoodie, but Frederick didn't turn around. He was writing something on index cards spread in front of him. His video camera was on the bar, pointed at him, its red light on.

"Poor old Frederick," said Christine.

"You wouldn't do him, would you? I think no friends, it has to be, none of my guy friends."

"Of course not. None of my girlfriends either."

"So where would you get your guys? Who do you want to do? I am fascinated by this. I want to know everything. I want to know what it is you want to happen—you want romance, you want a nice date and a guy who pays attention to you, or you want—"

"Jesus Christ no," said Christine. "I want a twenty-one-year-old. Or a nineteen-year-old. I don't care if he even talks."

"Jesus."

"Is that sick?"

"No. No, it's not sick. It's a little frustrating."

"Frustrating?"

"Well, just sad that I want to do you all the time, like every day and every night, just like a nineteen-year-old, and you don't seem to want that."

"That's not fair. That's not." Christine sighed and was unable to come up with anything else, or so it seemed to Dominic who was vindicated.

"I get it," he said. "I get it. It's not natural to stay with one partner for so many years. Believe me, I get it. I can't believe we are finally admitting this." He caught the glance of the elf, who was rushing by, and the elf actually bared his upper teeth as if snarling. "I would want to know every detail of it, though. Everything, including technical specs like hydraulics, displacement."

"You are threatened by the nineteen-year-old. I don't know if I could do it anyway."

"Even I wouldn't do a nineteen-year-old."

"Okay, so tell me who you would do? You'd go to your exes, first, I guess."

"I guess." Dominic slumped a bit, eased the tension on his right buttock, and then let the pain shift from his outer to his inner thigh. His exes were all almost as old as he was now. Concetta Accoglienza was much older. Although she looked like perfume itself over there in her black lace dress and her chingling bangles and necklaces. She was showing a lot of faintly lined breast. "But I want to know about the nineteen-year-old. Would you just approach one on the bus?"

"I don't know when I'd take a bus."

"Well, see, you'd have to."

"I would ask Helia for one of hers."

"Helia. What do you mean, one of hers?"

"Oh, since the divorce, she's been on a tear. I don't know where she meets them. Online, probably. It's all very casual, it's just hookups."

"No way. How, where do—" Dominic was picturing Helia, her vast breasts and her maternal way with him, as if he were Christine's little brother. "Helia? Are women like this now? How did I miss this?" He supposed Christine herself was once like this, at the time when he had met her. "So it's Helia who's inspired you, right? I get it. You've been hearing her stories. You're envious of her freedom."

Christine shrugged. "I guess. Yes."

"Well, me too."

She sighed. "We need our drinks now."

He said, more gently, "It's the meeting and the dating that I'm scared of. It just exhausts me, the idea. All the spending and the waiting and then the tearful phone calls. And then meeting for coffee to apologize and be friends."

"Oh god yes," said Christine. "I have no interest in dates. And that's probably the scariest thing about it. I'm not afraid someone would get weird in bed or pull a knife on me. I just don't want him to send me a fucking poem the next day."

"Ha." Dominic tried to remember if he had sent Christine any poems, early on. Of course he had.

"Look," she said, "the whole thing is embarrassing, I know. I can't stand to hear people talking about dating. You know what they mean by dating? People say they are dating when what they mean is they took each other's clothes off. And there's something always a little embarrassing about that. They saw the other person's squidgy genitals and breasts and hairs and then they touched mucous membranes, and they were excited and disgusted by this and wondered if they had to do it. When you say dating you make a picture of restaurants and glasses of wine. Dating is actually tasting someone's genitals and trying to make them come. We should call it something more accurate."

"Wow." The cocktails were finally there. Dominic grabbed his, a murky amber tumbler with some kind of brown berry floating in froth at the top. It was sweet and bitter, like all of them.

The little waiter tried to remind them of what they had ordered. "So this is your Smokedrop, with the lingonberry, and the white—"

"Thank you, thank you. We're fine." The waiter turned quickly.

"I agree with all this," said Dominic. "It's a very strange thing. We should call it something more honest, it's not dating, dating isn't what it's about. We should call it something that represents the most medical of nakedness, the exposing of the most private processes, like witnessing diarrhea. We should call it shedding. We should call it moulting."

"Yes," said Christine, "I am moulting with him, you would say, and people would look away, like you said I had a colonoscopy."

Dominic laughed in the flash of pride he often had when Christine was on a roll; he wished his friends were around to see it, even Frederick should come over and be reminded. He said, "Should we ask Frederick over for a drink?" Then, "Do you want to do Frederick?"

"It would be too sad to do Frederick."

"Oh, he's not sad. He's doing fine. Look at him, he's working."

"What does he work on? What does he work on all the time? What does he live on?"

This was a question she had been asking Dominic for years, and he still didn't know, so there was no point in answering, which was fine, because another tiny waiter was on them, calling them guys and telling them about braised cabbage and pork brine and Northern Ontario pickerel and then informing them, once they had made their basically random choices—Dominic and Christine didn't care about food all that much—that it was all good.

"So," said Christine, "it's all good. Or is it? You don't really want to do it, do you? I thought you were so frustrated, you said yourself, predictable, our sex life has become *so predictable.*"

"Yes, I do want to. I said so years ago and you freaked out, no, no, don't say you didn't because I recall it exactly. So yes, I want to try it. I'm amazed that you want to. I'm just trying to process it. I would have been terrified to even suggest it to you. And I was always getting in trouble for staying out too late and having coffee with exes."

"There was a lot of coffee with exes. A lot. Here's Frederick."

Frederick sat heavily on the banquette beside Christine. He did not look at them because he was looking down into the upturned screen of his video camera, as he always did. Frederick had not shaved in a few days and had had a cigarette very recently. His glasses were so thick one could never really see his eyes, except as giant projected eyes on small convex screens, like the mouths of fish in a bowl. "Tell me," said Frederick, "what you are thinking right now." The camera was pointing at Dominic.

"I am," said Dominic. "I am wondering. About something. Something to do with my wife." Dominic turned away and wrenched his hips again so that he could stare at Concetta Accoglienza's daughter as he spoke about this. He said, "My wife has suggested to me that we have an open relationship."

Frederick did not look up from his screen. He never did. This was his trick.

Concetta Accoglienza's daughter—Dominic had met her, once, and should remember her name—Nicola, or something like that but with one more syllable, Eleganza, Fantasia, Porphyria, Cryptomania—was an unnatural redhead with cleavage. She had no jewellery on and possibly no makeup either. She sat erect and smiled at her mother and did not look at him, as of course she wouldn't as she was only twenty-four or something, born when Dominic was already cheating on women he had been living with.

"I don't know if she is being really serious about this," he said to the room, "or if it's just a titillating game, like the game of Who would you sleep with or which of my friends is the hottest that we used to play in our twenties before we all got scared off such games because they are evidently dangerous. It is a fun game and we don't have to actually follow through on it." He was aware that he was speaking as if before a class, and that this tone and manner could be irritating to his friends, but he couldn't help himself, he enjoyed it. He did not glance at Christine's face, he didn't know how she was taking this and didn't want to know. "The rules of this kind of relationship," he said evenly, "are easy to figure out but less easy to implement. For example, we could have an agreement that we tell each other if we have some new partner in mind, fine, I think that's what we would have to do, but the evening would come, the day of the date, and one of us, say my wife, would say, okay, I'm going out now with Raoul, you haven't met him, he's twenty-years-old, because we've agreed that nineteen is too young, have we not, and okay, he's twenty-years-old and he's six-foot-three and he doesn't speak English very well, and I'll be out all night, so don't wait up. So then the other partner, say me, stays up all night, after having watched a lot of porn and trying very hard to get to sleep in various ways, and then is very sad and angry in the morning. I just don't see that working either way."

Christine spoke now. "Some of us are already used to that."

Dominic sighed. "Frederick, you have hours of us talking like this, ten years, at least, of us talking like this, of everybody talking like this, what do you do with it?"

"The point is not what I do with it." Frederick was panning the room now, slowly. "The doing is this. The point is the doing."

"Is it all posted somewhere? Is it stored at least?" said Christine.

Frederick turned the lens on her. "It's all stored and archived," he said to the camera. "And you've seen excerpts of it in my gallery shows."

Christine and Dominic were silent as they thought of Frederick's shows, the dark galleries with the projections on the walls, static shots of corridors and parking lots and subway tunnels.

"I edit out all the dialogue," said Frederick, helpfully.

"Aha."

"You should shoot Concetta Accoglienza," said Christine, "she's over there."

"The art lady?"

"And her daughter," said Dominic, "Glossolalia."

"Wow, she wears a lot of makeup." Frederick got up. "Where you guys going after?"

"Oh we don't go anywhere, after," said Dominic, "any more. This is it for us. You?"

"There are some folks going to Petunia. Not till later."

"Wow, Petunia. I've heard about it."

"You haven't been? Oh, you should." Frederick was nodding very slowly and deliberately. "You definitely should. Petunia is very well . . . stocked."

"Stocked," said Dominic. "I can only picture that."

"Oh, stop it," said Christine, "you are not dead. I would love for you to go to Petunia. With Frederick. Go. Have a great time."

"You are kidding me," said Dominic.

"You guys work this out," said Frederick, and walked away, his camera at his waist, aimed at Concetta Accoglienza and her daughter, who had just pulled her hair from her band and shaken it out over her shoulders. She had quite a lot of hair.

"You can sleep with her, if you like," said Christine, "Catatonia. She's beautiful. If Concetta Elaboranza Laborobora wouldn't mind."

"Oh right," said Dominic. "You know what I look like to a twenty-year-old girl? First of all, I don't look like anything, because I'm invisible. But if I do happen to cross her vision, somehow, because perhaps I am teaching her a class or she is introduced to me as one of her mother's friends, what she would see is actually not a man at all, but a symbol representing authority figure. A symbol, a cipher, like a one of those, what do you call the signs on bathroom doors? Ideogram. It's like when you see a guy in a red Santa suit. You just see the suit. You just see Santa."

"You look like Santa to her."

"I am Santa. I am some kind of person, an authority figure, but I have no body, I am just a brain in a tank, I am completely devoid of any sexuality or any physical component. Especially since . . . Speaking of Santa, would you do the elf?"

They watched him then, the elf, who was barking something at a chef behind the kitchen bar, and grabbing two plates with his claw-like hands and stalking with them, every tendon on display, through the tables where he was watched as one might watch a juggler or mime.

"I might," said Christine.

"Are you joking?"

"He has it. He has that thing. That mean thing. That's all it takes."

Dominic watched him slam the plates down and saw it, he saw that thing. "You wouldn't get a poem from him."

"Exactly."

"How would he climb you? Ropes and things. Pitons. It would hurt."

"Yeah but he would whisper incredibly vile things in my ear in a squeaky voice."

"So he's not really a small man but rather a large penis."

"I think so."

"A spiky penis."

"See I'm all turned on now." She said this in a voice that was not turned on though.

Their food came, all brown and green and salty, and Dominic found he was very hungry for it, which he never used to be, he remembered, when they were out so much more often. He was eating more and drinking less. "I'm eating more," he said.

"That's good, that's good for you."

"It's sad is what it is."

"What, you're going to put on weight? You will never, ever put on weight."

"No, no, not at all. It's sad that instead of sleeping with all these young people we just go and eat their food. We eat their food and look at them. The less sex we can have with them the more we eat their food. And look at them. They're not eating their own food. They're working. And then they're going to get laid after."

"Do you think," said Christine, "that we're ghouls? Like we come here out of hunger."

"For their flesh. Excellent idea. I think it applies to anyone over forty who goes to a restaurant. They're just sex ghouls."

"Love the Sex Ghouls," said Christine. "First album, though."

Once a respectable portion of the salty food had disappeared, and all the wine, Dominic hoisted himself and began his prickling walk to the stairs to the washroom. If he had enough wine he found his gait was almost normal, aside from the unusual swing his left leg had taken, his foot like a ball at the end of a rope, and the tearing feeling, the feeling that something was being frayed with every step, was only on the forward step. The farther he walked, he hoped, the warmer the joint would get and the less noticeable this shredding would become. Although one of the neurologists had told him not to walk at all. That was a great idea.

The stairs were okay going down but would be full of stabs going up. The Mindfulness Advisor he had seen for four unreimbursed sessions would tell him not to think about that, about the pain of a few minutes hence, until it happened, as worrying about the future was the cause of all his, Dominic's, angst. Dominic said, "You fuck-ing prick," in the stairwell just as a girl opened the bathroom door and started up the steps. It was Concetta Accoglienza's daughter. She stopped, looked up at him. She was as pale as her mother. Dom-inic pretended to be humming a song whose lyrics were, "You fuck-ing prick, hmmm hmmm." He tried to make himself flat against the wall as she passed. Her eyes were down and she climbed quickly. Her hair brushed his face and it smelled like the first floor of a very forbidding white department store. It was not a good time to remind her that they had met when she was about twelve.

He hummed his pretend song all the way down.

When he emerged from a stall, there was Frederick at the stain-less steel sinks. The camera was on the counter, unblinking. "Hey," said Dominic.

"Hey."

Dominic washed his hands. He winced as he bent. "The source of all my angst," he said to the camera, "is not my inability to be in the moment but fucking pain. Actual pain. That is the source of all my angst."

"You should come to Petunia," said Frederick. "You haven't been out for a while."

"I've been under the weather."

"You look fine. You're fine."

"Christine wouldn't want to come."

"So come without her."

"Ah, that, as you know, is not the easiest—" ·

"I have." Frederick produced a small rectangle of folded paper from his pocket and waved it. "The groove." He began to open it.

"No, no," said Dominic, staring at its contents. "No. Can't. I'm on all these pain killers and I just don't, I don't any more."

"That's cool," said Frederick. He went into a stall and closed the door.

Dominic waited, he wasn't sure why. He stared at himself in the mirror, a narrow man. Drawn was the word. A drawn man. He waited for the sound of the long sniff. He was going to go right back upstairs. "Am I Santa?" he called, "or an elf?"

Frederick emerged. "I left a little bit for you. Just a touch."

"Christ," said Dominic, "no."

"I'd rather be an elf."

"A fucking angry elf. Yes."

Frederick picked up his camera. "You will enjoy Petunia."

Dominic went into the stall.

When he had clambered up all the stairs, grimacing, he was breathing hard. He went to the coat rack to get his cane before he went back to the table. He walked more confidently with the cane.

"I asked for the bill," she said. "You all right?"

He sat and breathed. He said, "Were you really encouraging me to go out with Frederick after?"

"Why not?"

"Why not? Why *not*? Because not just a year ago you would have been frowning and sighing right now and asking me what time I would be home and who would be there, meaning what women, and making me promise I wouldn't do any lines and to call if I was going to be late."

"That's just bullshit. Is that really how you see me?"

"It is not bullshit, it is not even a slight exaggeration. You would have done everything in your power to discourage me from going to some place named Petunia with Frederick. It would have been like asking you if I could go to a hotel in Casablanca with Dominique Strauss Kahn."

"I would go to a hotel in Casablanca with him."

"What is going on with you? Do you have a date? Already?"

"I'm happy to go home. I want you to go out. Have some fun. It will be good for you."

"Wow."

"And I don't mind if you are doing lines with Frederick."

"Oh, no, he doesn't, any more."

Christine stood up, pushed the table towards him so she could slide out. "Don't even try that on me. I can see you did a line with him right now."

"What are you talking about? Don't be ridiculous."

"Oh stop. Who cares. Can you get our coats?"

Dominic snapped upwards. He crossed the floor almost without his cane. His hip was electric but in a not-intolerable way. He was overheating. He got the coats and helped Christine with hers and they called their thanks to the kitchen and the host and the elf. The elf stopped what he was doing, leaned against the bar and looked at Dominic. He opened his mouth and jerked his nose upwards. Then he stared a second longer and turned away.

"Okay," said Dominic. Then he turned to Concetta Accoglienza's table. She saw him and wrinkled her eyes. She waved.

"Go over," said Christine. "Be nice."

"Christ." Dominic stretched his face into a rigid form he hoped would come across as more smile-like than electrocution-like, and moved through the tables. Concetta's hair was black and shiny; everything about her was brilliant, except for her skin which had gone dry and papery, overnight it seemed, although it had been more than a year, probably, since Dominic had seen her.

"Sweetie," said Concetta. "What happened to you? Did you fall at a rave?"

"Yes," said Dominic, "I climbed on top of the speaker stacks. Thought I could fly. You know how it is."

"Really?"

"No. It's nothing serious. Hello," he said to the daughter, and looked down at her chest, which was different from Concetta's.

"You know Constantina."

"Indeed, we met many years ago, you were only small."

The daughter smiled. "My mom talks about you all the time." Her hand was hot.

"You really had me fooled about the rave," said Concetta.

"Concetta, there aren't really raves any more. Are there, Constantina?"

"I wouldn't know. I just study all the time."

"Constantina's at Brown," said Concetta.

"Brown, wow. Brown. The birthplace of the rave, no?"

"Is it?" said the girl.

"No."

"Go," said Concetta, "you're keeping your wife." Concetta waved and smiled towards the door. "Tell her she's beautiful."

"I will."

"She really is."

"I know that. Nice to see you again," he said to Constantina. "We're off, well, I'm off, with some friends, to a place called Petunia. It's a new place and apparently it has some whatever. Some style. You're both more than welcome to come."

"Oh, I'm far too old for that," said Concetta. She extended her hand as if to look at her rings and bracelets. "This one might want to go."

"Is there music?" said Constantina.

"Oh I'm sure there is music. It's all music." Dominic glanced towards the door, at Christine waiting with her coat on. She was texting.

"I haven't been dancing for like ever."

"You should go. You've been cooped up with your boring old parents for days. Dominic will take care of you."

Dominic looked at Christine, who looked up from her phone. She raised her eyebrows.

Dominic was conscious of being watched as he took out his own phone and entered the number that Constantina dictated to him. Then he shook hands with the girl and kissed Concetta on her perceptibly powdered cheek and came back to his wife. She took his arm and helped him down the two steps to the freezing street.

The concrete was white from the light of Djibouti Cafe and Restaurant (Business Club). There were still guys in there, on display, smoking their hookahs, looking disapprovingly out at all the people who cared about getting into Petunia.

"Look at the Pharisees," said Dominic, "watching in judgement. Hey, did you see that look the elf gave me? It was pure hatred, like a challenge, it was what guys do when they want to fight you. It was like, you looking at me? Let's fucking do this. He is so fantastically in character all the time."

"I'm going to walk," said Christine. "You get this cab."

"Now that is crazy, really crazy. I'm coming home with you. Then I'll get a cab."

"You're not going to walk all the way home though. It'll kill you."

"It's exactly what I need," said Dominic. He put as much weight as he could on the cane and tried to stand tall. "Or we could get a taxi together, home, and then I'll go."

"Why?"

Dominic looked at his wife. She was tall on her heels, her head up, looking down the street for a taxi. Passing students looked down furtively at her calves in their shiny leggings. She looked like a photo shoot. People watching would have been jealous that he was taking her home. Except he wasn't. "I find this weird," he said.

"What? You want me to be all hysterical that you're going to a club with Cenerentola?"

He snorted. "That's good, Cenerentola, that's funny." Then, quickly, "It's not really a club. It's more kind of loungey from what I understand. But yes, I guess, yeah. I think this whole thing, this whole new idea." He had to stop talking because a car stereo was too loud. Wind sliced into his coat. He struggled to button it with one hand on the cane. "I have to admit, although I think it's not a bad idea, I have to admit it hurts my feelings." He was almost shouting this. "It hurts my feelings that you don't want to come home with me."

"Of course I do, sweetie." She stepped back from the curb. A cab swerved almost onto them both and stopped with a jerk. She opened the door. "But I know you don't. Go out, have fun, tell me all about it. We'll talk about the other thing later."

"Listen," he said. He was holding the cab door open. "It's not going to be forever, this leg thing, whatever it is. If it was life-threatening they would be more panicked about it. It's most likely something that will go away on its own and I'll be better, some time. I'm going to get better."

"Uh-huh."

"And then I will be more myself and I hope things will get back to normal, in every way, don't you?"

"Of course. Give me a kiss."

She slammed the door, and the cab sped away.

Dominic stood there for a moment to check his phone—there was indeed a text from Frederick, an address—and then stuck up his hand. Two taxis squealed to a stop and some honking followed.

He gave the driver the address. He listened to the Koran being recited. This had become a comforting sound. He watched the bright facades slicing by and the girls slipping on ice in their heels. The car got stuck in traffic beside a dark park where there was nothing to look at and the arabic chant grew irritating. *Cenerentola* was so good. Not everyone would get it, which was one of the attractive things about Christine.

When they reached the next light, Dominic leaned forward and told the driver they were going somewhere else. He gave his home address.

Dominic and Christine lived down a lane between two houses. It was known as a coach house although it had actually once been a garage. He got out of the cab on the street and walked down the lane. He walked past the front door of frosted glass. The motion-sensitive light went on. He walked around the side of the box, where there was a sliding glass door. Through this door, if the curtains were not drawn, one would be able to see into the entire main room, where both the kitchen and the television were. One would be able to see if anyone was home.

He stopped carefully just before the door. There was light coming out. He stepped back, just beyond the reach of the light, and peered in.

Christine was sitting on the sofa, in front of the TV. She was wearing her terry-cloth bathrobe, and black socks, and her reading glasses. She had a litre bottle of Coca-Cola on the side table, which was something she would not drink in front of him. She was knitting. The thing she was knitting was only small still, a woolly square, with two stubby extensions. Perhaps these were sleeves. She kept stopping and leaning forward, poring over some kind of instruction sheet laid out on the coffee table.

On the tv were the expressive and overly blonde women of the kind of reality TV show that Dominic could be withering about if he caught her watching it. One of them was trying on a wedding dress. The other women were reacting with a pantomime of hysteria. All of this was silent.

He watched her knitting. She was not very good at knitting—she had tried it in front of him, a few times before, after her friends had had babies—and scorned it just as he had. He watched her unravel several rows and screw her eyes up at the magazine and start again. She was being very patient with the knitting.

It was, as she turned the thing over in her hands, starting to look like a tube or sleeve, although a very tiny one. Of course it was a baby sweater, for the new one, Frieda's new baby, her second. It was a crazy thing for someone like Frieda, almost forty and single, to do, to have a second one; she had already been poor and exhausted enough by the first one. Dominic had commented on this until Christine had told him to stop.

Dominic did not know for how long Christine had been knitting this thing. At the pace she was going, it must have been for a while.

Dominic watched her a while, knowing then that he had to go back to the bars, that he could not interrupt her in this secrecy, could not admit to having seen it, everything that Christine was doing and wearing and hiding from him, and he felt a terrible longing to protect her, a tenderness, as if she were his small and only child.

"Research" was first published in *The Queen Street Quarterly*, "Fun Girls" in *Toro*, "TXTS" in *Lostmag*, "Confidence," "Gentri-fication" and Crazy" in *The New Quarterly*, "Sleeping With An Elf" in the *Humber Literary Review*.

THANKS

Jowita Bydlowska
Martha Magor Webb
Dan Wells
John Metcalf
Emily Donaldson
The Ontario Arts Council
Pepper's Café

The line about poets and croquet players in the story "Confidence" is from Christian Bök.

Russell Smith was born in Johannesburg, South Africa, and grew up in Halifax, Canada, His previous novels include *Muriella Pent* and *Girl Crazy*. He writes a weekly column on the arts for the *Globe and Mail*. He lives in Toronto.